Out of the Ashes

An anthology by Bingham Writing Group

Contents

Maisie...9
Ann Packwood

Festival..14
Pat Bassett

Christmas Carole...17
Desiree Fearon

The Letter..19
Maud Harris

Know your Onions..24
Ann Packwood

It was so Different...26
Pat Bassett

Frigid Woman..29
Maud Harris.

The Pod..30
Jan Parnham

A Level Playing Field......................................32
Maud Harris

Space..35
Ann Packwood.

Murmuration..38
Brenda Dobson

The Boat Trip..**40**
Jan Parnham

Telephone Blues..**43**
Maud Harris

Bertie...**48**
Jan Parnham.

Laughing Buddha..**51**
Maria Ng Perez

Fairy Cake...**53**
Jan Parnham

Victoria...**55**
Pat Bassett

Genesis...**57**
Desiree Fearon

Journey of Discovery..**59**
Maud Harris

Rare Beef..**62**
Ann Packwood

Steak and Onions.....................................,........….**64**
Ann Packwood

The Argument...,........…**67**
Pat Bassett,

Katys' Friends...............................,,,……....…**69**
Desiree Fearon

Blood and Fire................................73
Maria Ng Perez

The Kindness of Strangers................75
Desiree Fearon

The Red Dress................................79
Ann Packwood

Resistance is Fertile........................81
Maria Ng Perez

Up a Gum Tree................................83
Desiree Fearon

If I Ruled the World........................88
Roger Smith

A Smattering of Life or Death..........93
Brenda Dobson.

Mrs Hardcastle................................95
Jan Parnham

Rescue Mission................................98
Maud Harris

The Tree of Life..............................101
Jan Parnham

Confusion.......................................103
Desiree Fearon.

Phil Atelist......................................105
Maria Ng Perez.

The Egg...107
Jan Parnham

Alf..**111**
Desiree Fearon

My own Place..**115**
Brenda Dobson

Katherine....................................,.................**119**
Ann Packwood

The Fishing Boat..**123**
Maud Harris

The Future.. ......**128**
Jan Parnham

Mother Russia...**131**
Maud Harris

Copyright

Published by Bingham Scribes Publishing

© 2017

This book is sold subject to the conditions that it shall not by trade or otherwise, be lent, re-sold, or hired out or otherwise circulated without the publishers prior consent in any form of binding other than that in which it is published .

Copyright for individual contributions rests with the writers

Maisie

Ann Packwood

Mark stood with his back leaning against the wall of the Charity shop, looking out over the counter at the people browsing through the rails of clothes and shelves of ornaments, pottery, books and shoes.

He'd just completed a course in journalism at college and had sent his CV to various newspapers and organisations. It was now a waiting game, in the meantime hoping to hear that one of them would invite him to an interview. He needed something to pass the time and thought the charity shop would enable him to observe the many people who came in during the day. They could be a source of inspiration for the characters in the novel he was going to write.

People were in an out of the shop all day. The so called antique dealers, coming in looking for a snip which they could then sell on in their shop or on their market stall, for a big profit. Housewives looking for a bargain, or hoping to find a replacement item for something they had broken. The bookworms searching for that elusive best seller everyone was talking about, or needing guidance from the popular gardening and D.I.Y. books. Others, who were really down on their luck, and looked upon the charity shops as a way of life to clothe themselves and their families with cheap, good quality clothing.

However, no one resonated enough with him to engage them in conversation whilst they paid for their purchases and enable him to glean ideas for his novel. The work was not as challenging as he thought it would be. In fact, he was bored and let his mind wander to his mates and where they were going that evening.

During his time at college many an evening had been spent in the college bar. His right arm had had lots of exercise downing pints of beer and throwing darts, and he felt he was in good form for the night ahead. He was a member of the darts team at his local pub, The Welby, and tonight was a big night as they had reached the finals of the Inter Pub Darts League. They had eliminated ten other teams from the competition and although their opponents from the Rutland Arms were good they were not, he felt, as good as their team.

The Welby over the years had changed from the traditional beer and skittles pub, when it was mainly men who frequented the bars. Now it was a bright open plan restaurant with a beer garden, where women were encouraged to dine and drink their wine, and children too were now part of the modern family scene. But the majority of pubs in the area still retained their darts teams and enjoyed the friendly rivalry which went on between them. Over the years The Welby had won many trophies and awards. Their Ladies Darts Team was pretty good too, with their history also stretching back many years.

Mark was suddenly roused from his thoughts by a commotion by the door. A man was opening it wide to enable a lady in a wheelchair to enter the shop.

"Oh, no," he thought, "not another escapee from the care home down the road!"

Pensioners, or senior citizens as they now had to be addressed, were amongst the highest number of customers who came in to browse every day. He was sure they had nothing better to do than to shuffle around the town, in and out of the shops, getting in the way of people who had busy lives to lead and work places to go to.

His mind turned again to the evening with his friends, shutting out the noise of the shop.
Suddenly a voice broke into his chain of thought, "Excuse me young man, could you help me please." It was the lady in the wheelchair.

'Yes?' He smiled, as he slowly walked over to where she was waiting by a row of shelves displaying various items of china and pottery.

"Would you pass me that trophy, the one at the back of the shelf."
He looked, and tucked away behind one of the jugs was a medium sized silver trophy, standing on its black plinth. Taking it from the shelf he handed it down to her. As she reached out he saw a change come over her face. Her eyes became brighter and a smile played around her mouth as she held the trophy up and turned it round and round.

He made as if to return to the counter but she called him back, her voice sounding excited as she held the trophy out to him, "Look, look, it's my cup! Look at the inscription!"

He took it from her and read, Maisie Little. Ladies Single's Darts Champion. 1979

He looked again, "What! Darts Champion!'
Seeing his disbelief she chuckled. "Yes lad, that's me. I haven't always been in this wheelchair. When I was younger I played in the ladies darts team at The Welby, but old age brought its own problems. I now live in the care home down the road but I like to keep my independence and get out and about as much as I can. Some time ago, when I lived in my own home, I was burgled and

this trophy was one of the things taken. I've been looking for it ever since. It meant so much to me and that match was a hard one to win."

Mark had heard of Maisie Little. He had also seen her name etched on the Ladies Darts Championship Winners board in the bar of The Welby. The old timers still talked of the evening when she became the Ladies Singles Champion.

It was the best of three games and Maisie and her opponent from the Bricklayer's Arms were throwing dart for dart. Each had narrowly won a game. It was now the deciding game. The first player to reach zero from 501 would win the championship. Maisie threw her darts well, consistently decreasing the score by 180. Now it was her last chance. Her opponent had missed the board with one of her darts and Maisie knew that if she kept her nerve and threw her last three darts accurately she would be home and dry. The room went quiet as she concentrated. Her first two darts scored 130. She needed 50 to win. Aiming carefully she threw her last dart at the bullseye in the centre of dart board. This would give her a score of 50. Her throw was accurate and the dart bedded itself into middle of the bullseye. The room erupted with loud shouts and cheers. Maisie had won.
So this was the legendary Maisie Little. Mark looked at her with new eyes and didn't just her as a lady in a wheelchair, he saw someone who had once been young and vibrant, and realised they had something in common, the love of playing darts.

As the shop was about to close he asked Maisie if he could walk back to the care home with her and if she would tell him more about her dart playing days.
Approaching the care home he felt very apprehensive. He had never been in one and was afraid it would be all doom and gloom, after all the residents weren't young. The majority of elderly

people he had seen around the town needed walking sticks, wheelchairs or walking frames to get about so they weren't very agile either.

But he needn't have worried. Maisie used the security code to open the front door and guided her wheelchair through to the bright, cheerful entrance hall. They were immediately greeted by a smiling care worker.

"Hi, Maisie! Had a good time in town? Who's this young man you've brought to see us?"

Maisie made the introductions. "Mark's come to talk about my dart playing days."

"He'll have a lot to learn, then. When he's finished with you there are plenty of others here he can talk to who have led lively lives, believe me."

And so the seed was planted.

Maisie told him all he wanted to know. Not only that, but after his first few visits to see Maisie he began talking to the other residents, who were only too eager to tell him of their younger days. Days when they were young like him, full of life and energy, and they felt they could take on the world. Some of them did. The visits also taught him that young and old could come together and that behind those walking sticks, wheelchairs and walking frames were real people, people who had helped to shape the world as he knew it. In due course he had his first book published. Others were to follow when he told the world the life stories of the hidden gems lying behind the doors of a care home.

But none compared to his first book. It was dedicated to Maisie and told her life story. It's title? 'There's more to me than meets the eye.'

Festivals – Expect the un-expected

Pat Winters

Liz watched and listened, with a lump in her throat and tears of pride welling up in her eyes, as the last powerful note from Julie's trumpet rang out into the auditorium. As the resonating sound died and Julie lowered her trumpet, there was a momentary silence – then the hall was filled with clapping, cheering and loud whistles of approval. The other young participants of Bloombury's first Festival of Youth Music joined Julie on the stage and the appreciative sounds grew even louder.
It was over. All the pain and heartache that had led up to this moment seemed worthwhile – it had been a wonderful success.
Liz thought back to the moment Julie had burst into the room clutching the letter detailing the forth coming festival.

'Mum, Mum, I've just got to have a new trumpet. Mr. Dawson says I could play a big part in it, but I just MUST have a new trumpet so I can play my best. When can we go to Sheehan's and choose one, Mum? I've got to get used to it and I've only got eight weeks. Can we go on Saturday? Thanks Mum. Just going to practise on this old thing until I get my new one.'

Julie dashed off in a whirl, leaving Liz reeling from the shock. Since she had been left to bring up her daughters alone, things had been hard, especially where finances were concerned. She had always tried to make sure they had not been disadvantaged because they came from a single parent family – but this was a step too far – trumpets worth their salt cost a fortune. She hung her head in despair and wished Julie wasn't so unreasonable in her many and continual demands.

The clocked ticked. Julie blew out tune after tune on each instrument in turn. She spoke to the salesman after every rendition, but Liz noticed her daughter didn't look particularly pleased with any one of them. Two hours later, after much waving and gesticulation on Julie's part, she flounced past her mother and out of the shop.

A brief conversation with the apologetic shop assistant told Liz that her daughter didn't consider any of the instruments up to the high standard the festival required and so she would have to withdraw.

Liz feared going home. She knew Julie would be in a foul mood and that she would twist it all round to be Liz's fault. She was not wrong on either count. The next couple of days were agony – that is until THAT phone call late at night on the second day. Liz had wearily answered the phone to an excited shop assistant. He had apparently felt sorry for Julie and had contacted a few professional clients who used the shop on a regular basis. He had explained the situation and had eventually drawn the ace card. Quentin Iron-Parkin had been considering taking a step back from his professional commitments and on hearing Julie's story had offered to lend her his best trumpet to play in the festival and would talk to Liz after the event if she wanted to buy it at a discounted price, providing Julie did it justice at the festival.

Julie was beside herself the next morning when Liz told her about the phone call. The next seven weeks drove Liz mad. The walls had vibrated to the sound of the trumpet for what seemed like every second of every day. Julie had been unbearable to live with as the concert drew nearer and Liz had unashamedly tried to make herself scarce. Now, thankfully, it was all over.

'Hello, Liz,' a voice cut into her thoughts.

'Quentin, you made it!'

'I sure did. She nailed it big time didn't she?'

'I'm very proud of her,' Liz replied, 'we need to talk about the terms for me buying this trumpet from you.'

'I've been give it some thought,' Quentin replied seriously.

Liz felt the lump in her throat again. She visualised weeks of tantrums if Quentin had changed his mind and wouldn't sell the trumpet after all.

Quentin cleared his throat and continued, 'I'm going to go into semi-retirement. I've always wanted to support a young up and coming trumpet player but I hadn't, until now, seen anyone suitable. I would like to give Julie the trumpet, take her under my wing, and point her in the right direction for a professional career.'

Liz looked at him, speechless. What a festival this had been! She couldn't believe her ears. Her daughter had the chance of a career of her dreams. The first music festival at Bloomsbury would be forever etched in their lives.

Christmas Carole

Desirée Fearon

She was awake, she had been asleep and now she was awake.

This didn't frighten her. She knew that she had done this before. How often or how many times she didn't know.

She knew nothing of time, only of now. Now she was awake. Things happened when she was awake. She remembered, or thought she did, if she could think at all.

She lay on her side, where she had been left, curled up and immobile, but breathing softly.

She tried to move her arms but they were close to her sides. Fastened down, wrapped around with something, she didn't know what or how, only that she could feebly flap her hands, and grasp her hands and pull at them inside the wrappings. She did this for a while, and then rested. She was so tired.

When she was rested she did nothing. What was there to do? She still could not think. She had no memory. Then she moved her legs. She had tried this before, she was sure. Stretching her legs against the bindings and bending them again and flexing her feet, rubbing them together, so that they became warm. She knew warm and she knew cold. She knew if you were one you weren't the other. She knew something then.

She opened her eyes. She could not see clearly, all she saw was a rectangle of blurry light. She knew light. She had seen shapes and lights. She did not know why sometimes she saw them and at others she didn't. Once one had been so bright, she had tried to turn her head away. She had closed her eyes so as not to look. She had cried out at it and it had gone away. It was not there. It was there and then not there, like sleep.

Now she saw more lights, they were different, they moved, and were not the same. They were interesting, and again they were there and not there and then there again, but quickly – not like sleep. She watched them for a while and then closed her eyes. She did not understand.

She could hear the noises of her body, but she was aware that when she slept, she did not hear them. When she woke up sometimes other noises filled her head, as they did now; good noises, low rumbles, beats in time with her body rhythms, in her head and around her, calming, soothing her. She liked this noise. It was not like the other sounds, the ones that were loud and sharp, that vibrated her and shook her and terrified her so that she tried to curl up away from it. Now was all peace, and softness. She was content.

Slowly she had a feeling inside her. Movement. It got stronger and more urgent, as if something was trying to escape. She felt a rush and a warmth in her lower half. What had she lost and why? She let out a piercing scream, and screamed and screamed. She was terrified.

Something lifted her, gathered her up into a warm place, made familiar noises, and moved her into the light. It unwrapped her and re-wrapped her, placed her upright against itself, and moved her to another place. She still cried. She wanted to fill the void that had been left in her. She moved her head around until she found a source of solace and settled down, again. Soon with her innards warm and full, she fell into a gentle sleep.

Alice laid Carole into the Moses basket in the middle of the room. She covered her over with a Santa-themed blanket. Her Mother said smiling at the baby,

"I can't think of anything better for a Christmas present than a brand-new granddaughter."

The Letter

Maud Harris

Emmylou is a professional spinster, a hater of men. Cocooned in her virginal bed, too tucked to move.

'Thou shalt not' embroidered above her, she despises everything that doesn't conform to her narrow view of how things should be. She lives alone in the small terraced house where she was born. Her job as a librarian is the only outlet she has, books are her friends, their smell and feel of them always brings her pleasure.

Having looked after her parents until they died within weeks of each other, Emmylou is suddenly without a sense of direction. Freedom from their increasingly petulant demands leaves a vacuum; she is frightened. Retirement looms. How will she spend her time? Her library desk has always acted as a protective barrier between her and the general public. How will she survive without it?

Many years ago a young man rode over the horizon, on a motor bike, not a dashing white charger. Emmylou was totally in love for the first and only time in her life. Strange and disturbing urges swamped her; she knew these feelings were wrong, but there was no one to tell her what was normal and what was not. She confided in the only person she trusted; Aunt Carla.

Aunt Carla was worldly wise and exotic, a complete contrast to Emmylous's mother; it was difficult to believe that they were sisters. With her flowing dresses and tousled blonde hair, Aunt Carla embodied everything that Emm's mother was not.

"It's perfectly normal to have these thoughts, darling."

Aunt Carla could always sooth away her fears.

It was with some trepidation that Emmylou brought her young man home to meet her parents. Their reactions were usually negative, and this time it was no different. The couple sat there in tense silence as Emm's father hurled a barrage of questions at him.

"Now, tell me my boy, what do your parents do for a living?"

"My father is a carpenter, Sir, and my mother keeps house."

"Have you always lived in Surrey?"

"As long as I can remember."

"Do you have brothers and sisters?"

"No, Sir, just me."

"Do you have a job?"

"Of course, Sir, I am a trainee accountant,"

Alan breathed a sigh of relief as they left the house.
"Is he always like this?"

"Usually, but this time he was even worse."

A week went by without a word from the young man. Emmylou was puzzled. Had her father really scared him off? His phone always went to voicemail. After another week a letter arrived at her house.

'Dear Emm.
Please forgive me. You know I am very fond of you, but with my studies and everything going on at the moment, I can't commit to a relationship. I hope you will remain my very dear friend.
Yours, Alan.'

Emmylou was devastated; she locked herself in her bedroom and cried for a week, resisting all entreaties to come out. Gradually, a new Emm emerged – a cold and resigned one. What was the point of allowing ones self to feel, only to have those precious feelings dashed. In future there would be no more vulnerability, emotions only led to hurt, so she wouldn't let them hold sway.

And so it remained.

Let us move forward some forty years. Emmylou is coming to terms with the loss of both her parents in a very short space of time.
 Now that the funerals are over and all the goodbyes' said, she begins the almost impossible task of clearing out a lifetime's clutter. The attic has always seemed a forbidden place. Emm climbs nervously through the narrow opening into its dark interior; the ladder seems precarious. Dusty cobwebs hang from the beams and she recoils as a spider runs over her foot. Stacked in a corner are piles of old newspapers, and behind them are several cardboard boxes piled one on top of the other. As she throws the newspapers down to the floor below, the dust cloud makes her cough. Old wireless parts and electrical plugs are thrown haphazardly into the boxes. Moving aside the largest one, carefully avoiding more spiders, she sees the glint of metal. Uncovering an old trunk, Emms' curiosity is aroused.
As she opens the trunk Emmylou feels that she is snooping on someone's deepest secrets. She imagines her parents watching her. Looking over her shoulder; with beating heart, Emm slowly lifts

the lid. Casting aside old legal papers, she uncovers a bundle of yellowing letters tied up with ribbon.
Emmylou is hooked.

Sitting down on the dusty floor of the attic she opens the first letter. It is addressed to Fairfield Adoption Agency. Inside the envelope is another sealed letter :
'My dearest boy.

You will by now know that you are adopted. I need you to know that it was never my decision to let you go. I hope and pray that your adoptive parents will love you as much as I do. Although I may never be allowed to see you, you are never out of my thoughts. Yours with affection .
Your mother.'

Emmylou gasps. This is too much to take in; that her cold and austere mum should have had a love affair. Emm can't quite believe it. With resolution now, she knows that for her peace of mind she must find out more. The only person left alive who might know the background is Aunt Carla.

Aunt Carla is old and frail, but she greets Emmylou warmly. A shadow passes over her face as she sees the letter.

"My dear child. I don't know how to tell you." Aunt Carla hesitates.

" Tell me everything, I need to know,"

"You may not like it, are you sure?"

"Of course. It's all in the past; I wasn't even born."

The story that Aunt Carla reveals leaves Emm in tears.

"It was wartime, your mum fell in love with a soldier; she was just seventeen. After he left to go back to the US, she found out she was pregnant. Things were different in those days, unmarried mothers brought shame on the family, they were stigmatised and shunned by society. Our parents forced her to have the boy adopted; it broke her heart and she never really got over it, even when you came along.

"Did she ever see him again?"

Aunt Carla hesitates, not quite looking at Emmylou.

"Only once, when you brought him home, eighteen years later."

I Know my Onions

Ann Parnham

I love my potting shed, I'm in most days and I'm always pottering about in my garden, pulling up weeds, staking up the drooping flowers. There's always something to do, and it keeps me out of the way of the wife.

I love my vegetable patch too. It's only tiny, but there's enough veg. to keep me and the wife going throughout the year.

My wife, she's an avid storer. Storing anything and everything, she won't throw anything away. It gets me down I can tell you. In the house there's never anywhere to sit because all the chairs are covered in papers, books, knitting and sewing. Even the rooms upstairs which are not used now, the kids having left home, have become storage units. I keep on at her but she won't listen and still keeps adding to it all.
That's why I love my potting shed. I get on with my garden and she gets on with collecting her bits and pieces and doing her cooking, which is her other favourite thing.

That's another thing that gets me down! There's only the two of us now and she cooks as if she's feeding the five thousand. Instead of making one pie, she makes six! One for now and the others for the freezer to use later, she says. I ask you, why can't she just make one at a time? We've already got two freezers full of food and the rate she's going it will soon be three. To me that's another way of storing. I tell you it's getting beyond a joke.

Mind you, I had a lovely crop of onions last year. Storing well they are, in my potting shed. The wife, she knows where they are, and uses them when she does her cooking.

The other day my old mate across the road asked me to go down to his allotment to look at the marrow he was growing to put in the agricultural show. Huge he said it was, and sure to win a prize. Well, I couldn't say 'no' could I?

So, when I finished digging up me daffs I put the bulbs to dry off in the potting shed and set off down the road.

He was right. It was a big marrow and we soon forgot the time through admiring it, measuring it, and talking over what the other competitors would be putting in the show. I said I didn't think there would be any competition from anyone else. No one could grow a marrow bigger than his.

"Better get back to the wife now," I said, looking at my watch. "She's doing Liver and Onions for dinner. My favourite."

As I went in the back door to the kitchen I could see the plate with my dinner, keeping warm on top of a steaming saucepan. I went through to the dining room, and there I saw the wife, slumped over the table, her head in her dinner.

The doctor said she must have got the onion and daff bulbs muddled up, 'cos that's what killed her so they said. She'd put the daff bulbs in with the liver, instead of the onions. Everyone said it was an unfortunate accident, and I agreed with them, but at least now I can find an empty chair to sit on when I come in from the garden.

And my onions and daff bulbs are in the places where I usually store them so that never the two shall meet.

It was so different last year

Pat Bassett

James was the son in law from hell. He had never exactly been sociable even when Stan and Liz had first met him, but his behaviour had got worse over the years. At Martha's christening he had threatened to pulverise his in-laws if they didn't vacate the village hall quickly. Why? Stan and Liz had never really understood - after all they had helped with the food, set up the hall, and done all the clearing up when everyone had gone. Granted, James had done the washing up, but then something seemed to flip in his warped brain and he had chased them out of the hall, screaming like a banshee across the road as they beat a hasty retreat to the car. Liz remembered it so clearly - the cricket team had been playing a match on the village green and they had all stopped playing, without exception, and stared at James, angry and screaming in the doorway.

Things had jogged along after that with Stan and Liz avoiding James whenever possible. Birthdays and Christmases were always difficult times. James refused to speak to them but turned on the charm to everyone else who appeared out of the woodwork on these occasions. Stan and Liz tried to take no notice and pretended not to be too bothered. All that really mattered were Martha and Melody. They were the most adorable girls ever. Melody was extra special, as Liz had delivered her in the back of the car. They collected the girls from school once a week and took them to the park. There they had a picnic and then went swimming. It was a day Stan and Liz looked forward to every week. The girls always battled to be the one who had a piggyback with Stan, while the other skipped along with Liz. Those were happy days.

The girls also loved the shopping trips with Liz and Stan. These always happened just before each birthday and Christmas and more often if they could find an excuse. Melody was particularly good at getting twice as many new clothes as was intended on these trips. She knew exactly how to wind her grandparents round her little finger. Martha, being younger, was not so subtle in her approach, but she was old enough to realise that she would get the same number of items as her big sister.

James had always treated his parents with disrespect. They appeared to be frightened of him especially when he shouted at them and controlled their buying habits. Self centred and selfish - James always put himself first. He always had to have the biggest computer, the biggest television, the latest 'boy's toy' and the newest car. His wife had to provide everything for the children and herself. She didn't seem to notice James was being manipulative, nor did it seem to bother her when he threw the odd punch in her direction - with two young children, bruises could easily be explained away.

Then in November, James's mother died. He saw the ideal opportunity to drive the final wedge between his wife and her parents. Everything seemed to play into his hands when Liz and Stan were struck down with a sickness bug and were unable to attend the funeral. James worked on his wife, persuading her that his in-laws were not nice people and not fit to see the children. Fearing the fist, she told her parents they were not welcome at the house and they were not to see the children any more.

Liz and Stan were devastated. Those girls had been their life from the moment they were born. They tried phone calls and texts but neither were answered. They waited. Christmas drew nearer. They waited. They had spent every Christmas with those precious grandchildren. Still no communication. What could they do?

Two weeks before Christmas they made a decision. They would go away. Stan had always wanted to go away at Christmas, but had equally been drawn to the grandchildren. So they booked a last minute room. They decided to leave the girls' Christmas presents on the doorstep and pretended they were Santa and Mrs Claus!

Christmas had indeed been very different. The entertainment at the hotel had been superb; the food was delicious with no cooking for Liz. The weather had been unusually mild and the Boxing Day football match on the beach between the firemen and the fishermen had been exciting and hilarious to watch - there seemed to be no rules at all! They had missed the girls like crazy, but they had enjoyed themselves and seen another side to the festivities.

Perhaps James, selfish, self opinionated and manipulative beyond imagination, had actually done them a favour.

Frigid Woman

Maud Harris

Dozen oysters? aphrodisiac
Failed to get me in the mood.
Horn of rhino, powdered, sprinkled
In my tea, it tasted stewed.

Romantic meal by candle glow
Dozen roses, red as fire.
Tempting pudding, filled with chocolate
Can't awaken my desire.

Still he tries, a valiant onslaught
When, oh when, will he deduce
That, in spite of his endeavours
I'm not easy to seduce.

Then, at last in desperation
Sudden revelation grips
All he needs to breach my drawbridge
Is a massive plate of chips.

The Pod

Jan Parnham

I climbed into my pod and made ready to travel.
To investigate was our new mission, and I was one of a group of seven people who had trained and worked very closely together. We had intuitive and enquiring minds, and worked well as a group. We were also telepaths, and used this form of communication on trips and in awkward situations; sending images and unspoken sounds to each other as we explored the new, small planet that had suddenly appeared.

For many years, we had lived and worked in our travelling house, our spaceship; the little home that supported us as we searched for new worlds, planets, even new universes.
Our team of seven were all in our thirties and we specialised in communicating with new life or energy sources that we encountered as we travelled in search of new discoveries.

As I set off towards a new planet, I was aware of its changing shape. As I approached, it seemed to get longer, and its colour, a golden yellow, faded into a soft yellowish green shade. Then I was almost on the surface, which looked like soft, curvaceous velvet.
Once I had landed, I sent my thoughts out to my team- mates, and almost immediately received back from them the same feelings and responses to the planet, as my own.

My thoughts were questioning everything I saw. The beautiful colours with ever-changing shapes. Fine lines of silver, like outlines of animals. No people, No plant life. No..?.
I could not hold the images long enough to draw a conclusion of

what I could see.

Instantly, I was in communication with the planet itself. It was a life energy of very fine particles that could suddenly group together. A huge number of particles that could create ever-changing sizes, shapes or colours, in whatever way it wanted, and then could almost instantly disperse and disappear back again, into minute, almost invisible, particles.

It could travel through space, and when it felt safe and at peace with the surroundings, would expand and grow into an amazing and beautiful planet.
Self-supporting and as united energy, it worked in total harmony, and would send out a universal feeling of peace. A feeling which would grow as needed. To the onlooker, it would appear as a positive being and be the colour, shape and texture of one's most precious memories.

It could also disappear in an instant!
Inevitably, the mind of man would start to question its usefulness to mankind. How it could be exploited, used and abused and eventually destroyed by the extraction of all its variety of life force.
Then, it would disappear.

◆◆◆

A level playing field.

By Maud Harris

The ice particles were fairy lights leading the way as I stumbled home. Slowly the dawn was breaking in the east, diffusing a pink blanket over the distant fields. Eyes glowed from a thousand night creatures, scurrying to their burrows as the day approached. The mountains were silhouetted as the sun slowly appeared on the horizon, A stillness settled over the land. The crunch, crunch, crunch of my footsteps echoed the beat of my heart as I pondered whether to tell the truth. Would I be believed? I had lied to Linda so many times before, surely I had used up all my capital; this time it had to be the truth – but how?
How could I admit a secret that would tear us apart? I couldn't lose Linda, yet I couldn't admit my shameful secret. Was it pride? Was it vanity?
The thought of losing her loomed like a giant bird of prey. I knew I wouldn't be able to survive without her. Linda had always been there, even when I was so steeped in self-absorption and self-pity that I couldn't see the way forward.
Oh yes! I resented her at times, especially when she took charge. At those times I felt belittled, less of a man, and I would hit out in frustration. But she had a way of restoring my confidence; sweetly, subtly her skills in the bedroom restored my self-esteem. I was her man, and boy! Could she seduce me out of my lethargy! Just thinking about her was beginning to affect me in ways that were melting the surrounding snow.
It was over a month now since the email. It came out of the blue, and hit me right in the gut. What kind of coward would sack someone by email? Not even the courtesy of a face to face meeting. How could I tell Linda? I imagined her reaction. Shock,

of course, and then she would be briskly optimistic and start pointing me in the direction of any number of unsuitable jobs. No! I couldn't face that. My solution was to say nothing and leave the house as usual, ostensibly bound for work. I would spend the day in the park if it were fine, or lurking round the art galleries and museums.

A month went by and I knew that the usual paycheque wouldn't appear in our bank account. How was I to explain that? Linda was one of those irrational women who set too high a store on truth. There was only one solution as I saw it.

The poker game was a regular Friday night feature, though I hadn't played since we married. The back room of the pub was small and dark; blue smoke drifted up and settled around the single unshaded bulb. It was warm with a comforting beer-tinged aroma. As we gathered around the scarred wooden table, Mike dealt the cards.

Right from the start I drew a good hand – I was usually lucky at poker, maybe it was my blank expression – my dead eyes, as the guys used to say.

I was riding high at midnight, and by 2 a.m. I was beginning to think I would be able to supplement our bank account. Two of the guys folded, leaving just three of us. By this time I was fairly confident, then BANG! Lady Luck did the dirty on me.

First my wallet was empty, then, in desperation, my car keys followed. The game folded at 5 a.m. and, carless, I was forced to walk the two miles home.

The wind rose as I trudged along the snowy track. The frozen droplets on the birch trees overhead tinkled like miniature bells. A single robin sat on a branch, its head on one side, reproaching me.

The glass panels of my front door loomed like a barrier. Normally I would feel a thrill of pleasure to be home – not this time. I was mentally rehearsing what I would say to Linda, but more worrying - what would she say to me? I held my breath as I stealthily inserted my key into the lock, not knowing what kind of welcome awaited me. The house was quiet, too quiet. Not a breath of air ruffled the curtains. No smell of coffee on the hob. Taking my shoes in my hand I crept upstairs. If Linda were asleep then maybe she wouldn't know what time I arrived home. That could work in my favour.

Like a wraith I crept into our bedroom. And stopped short. A beam of early morning sunshine fell across the room and alighted on the bed. It was empty, the sheets undisturbed.

After a heavy poker game and a long trek home through the winter landscape I was exhausted. Crashing out on the bed I was immediately asleep.

An hour later I awoke to Linda's key in the door. I heard the front door open slowly, then footsteps, barely audible, creeping up the stairs. There stood Linda, her high-heeled shoes in her hand. Guilt warred with defiance in her lovely face.

I seized my advantage.

"Where the hell have you been all night?"

Space

Ann Packwood

Our solar heated house was warm and cosy as the family, young and old, gathered together for our annual celebration. I looked around, we had come together from all over the orbit, one or two members just a step away but others taking the inter-orbital galaxy air shuttle, just seconds from door to door. We were not the only house having a gathering to give thanks for the safe deliverance of our many ancestors from the place we called earth, there were many, many more.

Over 100 years ago the people on earth knew that their planet was slowly dying. In 2015 the inhabitants of Carberet Islands in Papua New Guinea had had to abandon their homelands when the sea level rose, destroying buildings, crops and trees and contaminating wells with sea water. All attempts to build sea defences were washed away. The scientists knew that by 2100 with the melting of the polar ice sheets and glaciers, together with thermal expansion, the sea levels would raise the levels of earth's oceans by 5 feet displacing hundreds of millions of people worldwide, and they knew that something had to be done to save the human race.

In the late 20th century space travel was still in its infancy, there had been many explorations of space but finding another planet which would support the human race had come to nothing, the planets so far discovered would not sustain human life, and so the race was on to find a planet big enough for the exodus of people from earth.

Eventually, the scientists identified a planet, deep into space, they thought would be big enough, but would it sustain human life? Would there be water? Would the air be safe to be breathe? To find out it would need people who would take up the challenge to be the first humans to carry out this exploration.

My great- great- grandfather, Fred, together with his wife Sarah, were amongst the first to volunteer. They were young healthy newly-weds, just the sort of people needed for the venture and so, together with a group of other volunteers of all ages, backgrounds, and abilities, doctors, scientists and engineers, they boarded the first shuttle bus into space. Back at base the shuttle bus was guided towards the new planet, the scientists and boffins watching on their screens with trepidation and excitement.

The shuttle bus gently landed. A door at the side of the craft slowly opened and down the ramp came a robot to test the atmosphere and surrounding area and send back data to the craft, so that the scientists could analyse it and make a decision as to whether it would be safe for them to leave the shuttle bus. Reading the data from the robot it indicated that the atmosphere was conducive to human life and so the first volunteer to leave the craft came forward. It was Fred. To be on the safe side he wore a space suit which would enable him to breathe and as he walked down the ramp. He looked about him and saw in the distance green vegetation and a river. He walked towards the river and looked into the clear waters. Fish were gently swimming in and out of the rocks and he knew that life was sustainable. Gently taking off his space helmet he breathed in the pure air and turned to the shuttle bus, waving his arm indicating that all was well.

Over the coming decades the people from earth were evacuated and gradually built the new planet into a far better place than they had on earth. In 2100 the scientists were proved right. The sea levels did rise, swallowing up more and more of the land until the planet earth imploded on itself. But by that time The New World was well established and, one hundred years later, in 2115, we were honouring our predecessors who, through their bravery, ensured that human life continued.

Murmuration

Brenda Dobson

A Winter phenomenon, a movement in the sky.
Before dusk they spread along the horizon.
Thousands of black specks, swarming, parting,
forty or fifty birds, leaving then rejoining.

Continuous movement, waves foaming in the sky.
The colour of soot,
black fingerprints painting the sky.
To, fro, back, forth, swirling round and round.

                        Up and over and
                  back again,
an aerobatic display.
      Like a double helix of DNA,
Swirling, twisting,
        like birds in Thai Chi, and the
movement of waves and
      clouds,
                             chains in the sky,
    twist continuously.
                Ever moving.
    Ever swirling.

Gregarious starlings flock together in groups.
Migrants from the South join local troops.
Waves in motion, perpetual motion,
Asymmetric symmetry.

They swarm from the South,   swim   cross
the sky
as a whole,
not to reach the ground first,   not to be at
the edge.
Safety in numbers,   protection from predators,
then choose a place to feed,
and roost for the night.

Specks on the horizon, whispering, murmuring.
Reminder of the Civil rights Martyrs.
Poems of Freedom and staying strong together to
look larger than life,
for survival.

Enraptured I watch
I must capture this moment in words.
Waves in motion, rhythmical dancing in the sky.
Is this a way to spread the gene pool?
To meld the many flocks?
To branch out to even newer pastures?

Nature's mystery is not mine alone. No one knows.
A mesmerising sight. Fleeting moment of time.
Black Birds fill the horizon one moment, and are
gone to ground the
next.
I treasure that moment, its passage through the Seasons
and towards
the Survival of the flock.

The Boat Trip

Jan Parnham

We boarded the craft, the Brayford Belle, which was waiting, ready to receive us at the canal basin in the heart of Lincoln.
We climbed metal steps to the top deck, found our seats, which consisted of back-to-back wooden benches.
Our section was covered by a red canopy, to protect us from the 'delightful' English summer weather. It was a typical summer's day. Dull, slightly damp with a coolish breeze. In fact, very much a June day!
There was also a family of four on the top deck with us, plus the skipper in her cabin, ready to steer us on our adventure. Our boat trip was going to be a journey along the Fosse Dyke canal, which, so we were told, is the oldest in England and which eventually runs into the River Trent.
we glided along the water.
On the other side, a pristine private vessel was venturing in the opposite direction. A man at the helm was proudly steering with what appeared to be his family, behind him.
Gradually, we moved away from the hubbub of city life. We started to move. It was quiet, very gentle and smooth, as the busy bustle of people, cafes, traffic and noise, and gradually the canal became much narrower, with numerous house-boats moored to one side. A wonderful kaleidoscope of colours, shapes, sizes and styles, with many boats in need of repair.
One began to imagine how cosy the houseboats would be. Shutting the door and stepping down into a snug environment. Closing the small curtains and swinging your legs up on to a long, squashy cushion seat and perhaps then enjoying a glass of wine and a good book. Maybe even a box of chocolates! Leaving the hustle and

bustle of life outside and relaxing in a peaceful, restful place. No worries – at least until tomorrow!

The house boats were fascinating. Some were painted and cared for really well; one with potted plants in a row on the roof, filled with colourful pansies. On another sat a proud ginger cat, guarding the boat, and yet another had a bicycle attached, ready to scoot off for some shopping, maybe.

On the bank were a few washing lines, with garments blowing in the breeze.

Several of the craft had solar panels installed on their roofs, and many had a small rowing boat or dinghy tethered to the stern.

Along the banks was a selection of painted garden seats; either wooden or metal, waiting to be sat upon when the sun came out! The boats had names proudly painted on, Rosie, African Queen, and so on. The African Queen did look like a miniature version of the one in the film.

One of the boats had lovely painted flowers centred on each panel down the side. Another looked like a small, angular gun boat. Grey and austere. It would have been good to paint them as they were so different from one another. Each had its own character, and could perhaps tell many stories of life on the water.

Gradually, the number of boats lessened until there was just a towpath either side, with beautiful trees like mountain ash and weeping willows, and pink hawthorn in full blossom.

The banks were covered in delicate cow parsley, pink campion and bushes of wild roses. In the water were a great number of water lily leaves. No flowers, sadly, but water buttercups and tall iris leaves, with again, no flowers. It was still too cold for some of the flowers to bloom, but bird life was all around in the trees.

On the canal were drakes with their partners, moorhens and also swans with their cygnets, and seagulls hovered overhead.

Our guide said that the canal contained perch, roach, pike and eels, but we spotted none of them.

Suddenly the boat began turning towards the far bank then back, so that eventually we were facing the way we'd come.

We moved off past a small foot-bridge over a narrow river and saw the edge of the local golf club with its manicured greens stretching away. There seemed to be far more trees on this side of the canal path, but fairly soon houses began to appear. A few small, terraced houses at first and then larger homes and finally business buildings. In the distance, standing proudly on the top of a hill, was Lincoln Cathedral. Before the surrounding area became so built up, it must have been truly awesome, and even now is still a grand sight.

The trip back seemed much shorter than the trip out, but as we picked up our belongings and disembarked, we all agreed that it had all been splendid so far, and that a hot drink and a leisurely lunch would complete the outing.

♦♦♦

Telephone Blues

Maud Harris

Michael's Story.
As the train gathered speed I suddenly remembered, with a jolt of panic that Sophie had my mobile phone. I had handed it to her to hold while I loaded her luggage on to the train. I was all too aware that I hadn't input a password. Anyone could read the contents - texts, pictures, videos. My whole life was there on that phone.
   While there was nothing really incriminating, the fact that Sophie had access to my private thoughts was unsettling. That selfie of me in my underpants wasn't meant for general viewing, and what about the sexy text messages I had sent to Caroline from the office. There were a couple of girlie pics, too, that I would prefer not to share.

   My first thought was to phone her and ask her to return it, but wait! I didn't have her number, it was on my phone, but who can remember numbers that are not keyed in? If Sophie hadn't started on her gap year I could have contacted her, but she will be travelling for the next six months. My only hope is that she will contact me, but how?
   It suddenly dawned on me how much a part of my life my phone was. I thought at first that there was nothing really incriminating on it, but after spending a restless night tossing and turning I realised that was far from true. Even my Facebook entries were there for everyone to see.
   I wait for a week, watching the post every morning to see if she will return it. My sister suggests that I ring my own number. Why didn't I think of that; it's obvious, of course. I ring and get no reply though it rings several times. At least I have a way to contact

Sophie, but this only reinforces all my fears. What if she has accessed my data? My feelings of guilt grow by the hour.

Gradually as the weeks pass and there is no word from Sophie, and nothing in the post, I begin to relax. Maybe the phone is dead; maybe she's lost it. Six months later my sister reminds me.

"What happened about your phone?"

"Nothing really, anyway, I bought a new one."
This starts me thinking, I may as well ring one more time, for curiosity if nothing else. The phone is picked up at the second ring.

"Hello. Bangkok police station."
It's a man's voice speaking in heavily accented English. My breath catches in my throat. What the hell...?

"May I speak to Sophie?"

"Sophie no here, Sophie in jail."
The phone goes dead. I'm thrown into a panic. Here I am on the other side of the world; the questions race through my head. What has she done? Has she been framed for something? Most sinister of all - is it anything to do with my mobile phone?
My father is no help at all.

"You kids! You spend all day texting and tweeting, or whatever you call it. Don't you realise that anyone with a bit of technical know-how can easily access your details?"

'Tell me something I don't know!'
Dad suggests that I go to the local police station and ask if they can find out anything.

My heart is pounding as I approach the police station, in my mind such places are associated with low-lifes and criminals. I feel guilty even before I ring the bell. My words come tumbling out as I explain the problem to the desk sergeant, an older man, grey haired and overweight, his fleshy neck bulges out over his collar.

"Now, lad, let's summarise this, your girlfriend is in prison in Bangkok."

"Y-yes, and she has my mobile phone."
"What is she accused of?"

I feel myself flush, and say in a small voice "having indecent images on the phone."

"Speak up, son."

I repeat. "Having indecent images on the phone."

"Your mobile phone?"
I want to disappear, but force myself to reply.

"Y-yes."
He informs me that, as it is an international matter the British Embassy are the people to contact. He disappears into the back office, and after what seems a long time he comes back with a telephone number. I feel nervous contacting the British Embassy. This all seems so far over my head; I have no idea how these things work or even if they will believe me.

An official takes all the details, including the number of my old phone, and makes an appointment for me to come and discuss the problem. The following week finds me outside the British Embassy in London. Taking my letter of introduction, I present myself at the reception desk.

An aide escorts me to a large room with wood- panelled walls. A thick red carpet muffles my footsteps as I take stock of my surroundings. A dark mahogany desk is in the centre, with two leather chairs in front of it. A green desk lamp sheds a circle of light. A tall man in a grey suit rises to meet me. He introduces himself as Mr Eldridge, we shake hands, and he invites me to sit down.
"Now, let us start from the beginning. Tell me, in your own words, exactly what has brought you here."

I repeat the story that I seem to have told a thousand times over, and he nods like a wise owl. If I wasn't so scared, I would find it funny.

"Just one more question Mr Morton. Does your friend hold a British passport?"

I reply. "She was born in England and has always lived here."

"We will contact our ambassador in Bangkok, who will look into the allegations made against your friend. We take threats to our citizens very seriously."
He rises from his chair, proffering his hand.

"We will be in touch shortly. Goodbye, Mr Morton."
   A week passes in which I sleep very little, then I receive a phone call from the embassy. They confirm that Sophie has been arrested for having indecent images on her phone. She has alleged in a statement that I am the owner of the phone.
   The lady at the embassy is business like and calming. She tells me in a soothing voice that what constitutes indecent images in one country may not be so bad in Europe.

"Is it your mobile phone?"
   Totally embarrassed now, I reply.

"Y-yes."

"Now Mr Morton, what exactly is on your phone?"
I feel myself flush bright red, and I am thankful that she can't see my face.

"Just a few nude girl images and one of me half undressed. I keep my underpants on."
I say hurriedly.
She sounds amused.

"Well, Mr Morton, if you sign a statement admitting that you are the owner of the phone in question I think we may be able to close the case. You can do this at your local police station and we will contact them."
I creep into the police station hoping that nobody knows me. The same desk sergeant is on duty. I feel his eyes on me as I write out my statement, I'm sure he is laughing behind my back.
A month later I go to meet Sophie at the airport. She looks strained and has lost weight, but I'm still pleased to see her. I rush across to the arrivals gate and open my arms for a hug, she pulls away and I feel her tension; her expression chills me. Sophie hisses one word.

"Pervert!"
A month later I receive a phone bill for £600. For calls made from Bangkok.

Bertie

Jan Parnham

Jane had always thought of ghosts as something other people saw, until that is, she'd decided on the spur of the moment, to go for a short holiday to Wells-next-the-Sea, in Norfolk.
She'd been under a lot of strain at work, and that, plus some family issues convinced her that she needed some time away, somewhere to find peace and freedom and time for herself. She went on line and found a small cottage to rent, available the following week.
Jane picked up the key from a Mrs Roderick, a pleasant woman of middle-age, who lived just half a mile away from the cottage. She appeared quite well-to-do from her accent and demeanour, and was efficient and helpful, and gave Jane all the information needed for a comfortable stay.

Jane found the cottage charming in its chocolate-box style, with roses and honeysuckle around the front door and a small garden with a picket fence. There were many cottage-garden flowers and a wooden seat to sit on and survey the beautiful countryside.
Inside it was quite simple and homely, with all the basic needs for a holiday. Most of the house was painted blue and white and there were gingham curtains in most of the rooms. The exception was the kitchen which had primrose walls, a pine table, chairs and a Welsh dresser.

Jane unpacked her case and the food she had brought with her, and settled in, feeling quite happy and at peace.
Next day, after breakfast, she took her coffee and a book and sat

outside in the warm sunshine on an old wooden bench. No sooner had she sat down, than a golden Labrador came bounding up to her. Though friendly, the dog seemed rather agitated and kept barking and running to the gate and back. Thinking she might see the owner, Jane went to the gate, but no one was around.

She opened the gate and the dog ran up the road, looking back to see if Jane was following. When it realised she wasn't, it ran back and pulled at her skirt to get her to follow.

Thinking there must be a problem, she followed the dog up the road towards the first house. Mrs Roderick's house.

The dog rushed up the path and into the house with Jane following, now very worried what she might find.

At the bottom of the stairs was Mrs Roderick, unconscious but still breathing. The dog was sniffing all around her.

Using the telephone that stood on the hall stand, Jane dialled 999 and called for an ambulance. Telling her not to move the injured woman, they said that they would be there in ten minutes.

Those ten minutes seemed to last a lifetime, and during that time Jane and the dog kept vigil at Mrs Roderick's side.

It wasn't until the medical team had left in the ambulance with Mrs Roderick, that Jane realised the golden Labrador had disappeared, and though Jane enjoyed the rest of her holiday, going for long walks, reading, listening to music, and eating leisurely meals with a glass of wine in the local pub, she never saw the dog again.

Finally, she packed her bags on the morning she was leaving, loaded her car and said 'goodbye' to the lovely little cottage she had so enjoyed.

She stopped at Mrs Roderick's house to drop the key off, and was pleased to find that she was back home and fully recovered. She thanked Jane for calling the ambulance, saying she might have lain there until her helper arrived. Jane explained that it was the Labrador that had fetched her, and was startled when Mrs Roderick began crying, then said,

"My lovely dog, Bertie, died only a month ago. He was always at my side, guarding and protecting me. I do miss him."

Jane said "Goodbye," thinking it had been an eventful week. A week that had made her think again about whether ghosts do exist and whether loved ones ever leave you.

laughing buddha's words of wisdom

Maria Ng Perez

as you muddle through life

if destiny serves you diced serrano chillies

inflicting heart burn

& causing stinging tears

do not tread gingerly

blitz that recipe

& create something new

try 3 small pieces of fallen stars

with 5 oz. of five spice infused with dreams

add an oz. of freshly squeezed ideas

shake yourself out

& pick yourself up

over thawing ice

then add 1 oz. of fizz

as you pour

all that has lost its sparkle

down the drain

& remember

your glass is always full

if only with fresh air

cheers!

A Fairy Cake By Any Other Name

Ann Packwood

I was reading an article which said '58% of us tried baking in 2016, this is up from 27% in 2015'.

I noticed that the article said 'tried'. How sad I thought, 58% had only 'tried' baking. When I was young the figure would not have been 58% had 'tried'; it would have been 100%.

From early times people have baked. Archaeologists are always finding pottery dating back to Anglo Saxon and Roman times which had been used for making and baking dough in. It might not have been the cakes and pastries we associate today with baking, but it was baking, baking to put food on to the table to survive, although I am sure an enterprising Anglo Saxon or Roman wife did bake a treat for her family.

At school it was part of our school curriculum to learn how to cook everyday meals, and to bake cakes. Cookery lessons were held every week. Our mothers baked all the time and their knowledge was passed down from mother to daughter, and sometimes sons. With the coming of convenience foods, and cookery lessons no longer compulsory every week, this knowledge has not passed on to younger generations.

Cakes today can be rustled up from a packet – just add an egg to the mixture and pop in the oven. Readymade meals are easily available. So the art of baking and cooking with fresh ingredients has slowly disappeared.

Not in all families I am pleased to say. I did baking with my mother. When my son and daughter were young we spent many happy hours in the kitchen baking first, inedible cakes, and then as they progressed, cakes enjoyed by all the family. Later I enjoyed baking with my granddaughters and grandson.

The new fashion for cupcakes did come as a surprise. We have always made these in our family but they were called fairy cakes, rock cakes or butterfly cakes. My daughter still remembers making Rice Krispie cakes with her grandmother. So easy, and no cooking! Just mix melted chocolate with Rice Krispies, divide the mixture into little paper cases and pop into the fridge to set. How easy is that for introducing children to the art of baking?

If a new twist is given to an old theme and it will get more people, especially the younger generation baking, who am I to argue with this? Just let's have more cupcakes.

Thoughts of a Loved One

Pat Winters

Now the day is over

We must start again

Your soul has passed to spirit

Things will never be the same

You've left a gaping hole

Which we can never really fill

How can we ever swallow

This dreadful, bitter pill.

Life must go on without you

While in another world you rest

But knowing you, though not for long

Everyone was blessed

Though time will heal our sorrow

You will forever be

Near us and around us

Though we may not always see

The feather, dove or rainbow

That you send us as a sign

To show you are around us

And will be for all time.

Genesis

Desirée Fearon

This place is mine!
I am the great ice and I will flow for a million years across this land.
I am fire and rock. I am smoke, sulphur, and iron. I am the rising mountain. I have turned the ice to water. The water flows around my feet and I will rage for a million years.
I am nature. I am trees and moss. I am wind and rain. I am fish and worm and butterfly, and I am eternal.
We are the great animals, tall and wide. We walk with heavy feet. We eat the plants and the trees. We eat each other!
We are the small animals. We scuttle and hide.
We will survive!
I am MAN and this place is mine. I have changed the land. The mountain is now a hill – it has no fire.
I have built on it a place of worship - to myself...
I have taken the water and moved it and straightened its course. The water runs to my will now.
Trees grow at my instruction.
Plants are here, and roads and buildings, there. This is how I have ordered things. No creature stands in my way. Nothing is here but by my leave, be it animal, castle, or pavement. I am the great metropolis and I will rule forever.

I live in the hills. I live in the waters. I live in the trees and the flowers, next to the birds and the small things.
I live in the great beasts.
I live in the roads and the buildings, new or old.

I live in the places beneath the places, beneath the places that are long forgotten.

I am and I have been and will be again.

I cannot say what or who I am or who will rule here forever.

◆◆◆

Journey of Discovery

By Maud Harris

The woman sat at the window, deep in thought. To her left were her new neighbours, a young married couple. To her right she could hear the shrieks of laughter coming from two children playing with an old car tyre.

Staring into the middle distance, she reflected on the stages of her life – her voyages of discovery. Looking at the happy couple busily digging their new garden for planting, she cast her mind back forty years, almost to the start of the voyage. A young girl of eighteen, desperately in love with the tall, gangly young man. Together they had explored the boundaries of their love, new and magical for both of them. A short engagement before embarking on the sea of marriage, sometimes wildly happy, sometimes stormy. Would she change anything? Not for one minute.

Those first few years, they had called it Phase One. The carefree years before the children arrived, a time of getting to know each other, polishing the rough edges until they blended, each sacrificing a small part of their personality to the other, though both unaware of it.

Phase Two began with the arrival of little Lisa, and she turned their ordered world upside down. The woman was suddenly aware that she was responsible for this tiny life. She would stand over the cot looking to see if the baby was breathing. Waking up at 2am, in response to a bellow that could be heard a mile away, she would sleepwalk to the nursery and feed the infant. Two years passed and Lisa had a brother, Stephen, altogether a different experience. Stephen was what they called a 'good baby'. He slept when he should and ate at the right time. Life with two toddlers allowed little time for recreation, and even less for reflection. 'Where did those years go?' She asked herself.

It was during this time that the woman first began to question her role in life. In the long hours when the children slept and her husband worked, she would sometimes think back to when she was free to go out on the spur of the moment, to drive to the beach on impulse and just run on the sand. She wouldn't have said that she was unhappy, but there was a lack of something – an undefined loss. This she could never share with her husband, he would try and fix things. The slow process towards maturity could not be fixed. The years passed, nursery school then junior school, and more time for herself. A part time job where she felt valued. The woman supposed this must be the start of Phase Three, or was it Four?

It was Phase Five that engendered - was it guilt, or was it regret? - She couldn't bring herself to admit to these feelings. The experience itself was so energising, so compulsive; there was no way she could have resisted the affair.
It started innocently enough, help with a punctured car tyre from a work colleague, the occasional after work drink, glances across the room. Not that she alone had strayed; her husband had tearfully admitted to a brief liaison. Why, oh why must a man confess things better kept hidden? For her part she had kept her secret locked in her heart ready to be remembered in later years with nostalgia, but not regret.

The woman found herself drifting into a mood of sweet melancholy, and pulled up sharply, remembering that there were good times as well. Phase Six was a long one, lasting through teenage years, then seeing the children off to various pursuits. Worrying when Lisa went off on a gap year, then again when

Stephen bought a motorbike. The joy of grandchildren and the new mother and daughter closeness that was growing with their shared experiences. Then suddenly, it seemed, she was alone with her husband, whom she still adored after all their upheavals. The discovery of a quiet companionship and shared laughter as they sailed into calmer waters.

Then came cataclysmic Phase Seven. A sudden phone call. A collapse in the street. A dash to the hospital. All these things remembered and played over and over again like a recurring nightmare, though at the time her perception of events was blurred. The children were summoned and were in time to say their goodbyes. Then came the funeral and afterwards the disbelief and incomprehension, the questioning. Why? Why? Why? Then the anger, the bitter, all consuming anger with nowhere to direct it. Then came the tears. The long months when she wanted only to be left alone.

Acceptance came, and with it a slow, painful adjustment to widowhood. Slowly, slowly she reached the point where she could sit calmly and relish the good times they had shared. Bittersweet memories of their forty year journey. A time came when she could remember and smile; a move to a smaller house with a manageable garden and a beautiful view; neighbours who were friendly, involvement with a group of people of her own age who made good use of her organisational skills. She changed her car for a smaller model and explored the countryside surrounding her new home, a ten minute ride from the beach. Was there a Phase Eight? She didn't know, but for now she was content to drift.

Rare Beef

Ann Packwood

John called his dog, Shep, to heel as they walked towards the field where his prize English Longhorn cattle were grazing in the morning sun. It was a walk they took every day. When they reached the five bared gate leading into the field John stood as he always did, hands resting on the top bar looking over the herd, while Shep lay quietly at his feet.

English Longhorn cows are an ancient breed which came close to extinction in the middle of the 20th Century. While the horns of other cattle are usually on top of their head, the Longhorns are different, their horns sweep down either side of their face, almost reaching their nose. When you looked at them head on it was as if you were seeing them through a picture frame. It was this feature which had drawn John and his wife, Rose, to them in the first instance, that and the fact that they made excellent mothers, were docile and very easy to manage.

Feeling the warmth of the sun on his face and with bird song filling the air in the clear blue sky, John thought back over the years to when he and Rose had met at Agricultural College, many years ago. It was love at first sight. He was instantly attracted to Rose's striking looks, auburn hair, her sense of humour and eyes that twinkled with laughter, even when his jokes were not very good. She had been drawn to his rugged good looks, his face weathered to a smooth even tan through being out in all weathers on his parent's farm. She knew his character would match his hands, strong and capable. Their ambition was to buy a farm, with land,

and raise cattle which through one reason or another were almost extinct.

When they graduated money was tight. A rundown farm came onto the market, the house was almost derelict, but the land was excellent for their needs. With no money to spare, and to make ends meet, Rose created a vegetable patch at the side of the house and sold the produce at the local Farmers Market. In due course four children were born, three boys and one girl. The house was renovated and they prospered.

With careful management the herd increased and they now had a sizeable number of dairy cattle, and the Longhorns had come to play an important part in the beef industry. The vegetable patch was now a Farm Shop, selling their produce and beef to local discerning housewives who wanted to know the provenance of what they were buying and eating. The children were all grown up and doing well in their chosen professions.

So, all in all, as John stood looking over the herd he knew that life had been good, but tomorrow it would be a different walk with Shep. He and Rose were retiring to live by the sea. They had always thought one of the boys would take over the farm but none of them a shown the slightest interest in cattle. It was Lily, the only girl, who had gone to Agricultural College, learned all she could about rare breed cattle and tomorrow would be bringing in the Gloucester's. Nearly extinct, she had bought the last 33 Gloucester cows in the country at market and was determined to do with them what John and Rose had done with the Longhorns. She would carry on their ambition of breeding and rearing rare beef cattle, and with her knowledge of modern farming techniques take the farm into the 21st Century.

Steak and mushrooms

Ann Packwood

Muriel gingerly lifted the pastry lid of the pie on her plate.

"I thought this was supposed to be a Steak and Mushroom pie," she said to her husband, John, her voice raised an octave or two. "It looks more like gravy pie with a bit of steak and a lot of mushrooms floating about in it."

She lifted the pastry lid higher, and prodded the contents underneath with her fork, swishing them around the plate.

"What do you think? What's yours like?"

"I don't think it's as bad as yours, dear, but I see what you mean, there does seem to be more gravy."

Enjoying a day out to do their Christmas shopping Muriel and John thought they would have lunch before getting the final bits and pieces and going home.

"Go on then, John, complain to the manager. We've paid good money for this. It's a disgrace by anyone's book to have the nerve to put this rubbish on the menu."

Muriel was now getting on her high horse and her sense of grievance showed in her high pitched voice.

"It's not right! They shouldn't be allowed to get away with it!"

"Calm down, dear."

"Don't calm down dear me," she spluttered. "You sound like that chap who used to be on the telly advert. What's his name? Michael Winner? Call the manager, and show him what's under this pastry lid and ask him if he'd like to eat it."

"Alright, alright, just don't start going on at him when he gets here, I know what you're like when you get a bee in your bonnet."

"Is everything alright, Sir?"

Before John had a chance to say anything Muriel again lifted the pastry lid of her pie and looked directly at the Manager, "What do you call this?"

"It's our Steak and Mushroom Pie, Madam," he answered.

"Well, where's the steak and where's the mushrooms?"

Muriel was well into her stride now, I tell you it's a disgrace to put this on the menu to serve to your customers." Her raised voice was beginning to vibrate around the restaurant, causing the other diners to lift their heads to see what all the commotion was about.

"I'm really sorry, Madam. I'll take the pies back to the chef and have a word with him."

"You do that, and tell him he's ruined our meal."

Muriel and John sat stony faced staring into the distance and waited for the manager to return.

"I really am so sorry you have been disappointed with your meal," he grovelled when he returned to the table. "You must let us rectify this. Please, choose another dish from the menu, anything you like. Naturally, it will be with our compliments."

Muriel and John thoroughly enjoyed their meal of Rump Steak with all the trimmings. Fortified with a bottle of wine, again with the compliments of the management, they left the restaurant.

"Well, that was a good meal, Muriel." said John, as they continued with their shopping. "You know, you really ought to be on the stage, your acting skills are getting better and better."

The Argument - Jam

Pat Winters

"Your jam's in the way."
The remark hit Jack on the eardrum as he was eating his first glorious sandwich of the day. The strawberry taste activated his taste buds and he sank into a dream world. His mind often wandered to better things and better places these days as he sought a refuge from the aggravation and bitterness that surrounded him in the house.
"Your jam's in the way."
Still only a sideways glance, but this time the word 'jam' penetrated his consciousness. Ah yes, he recalled making the jam. How he had enjoyed stirring the hot, sticky substance as it bubbled and hubbled in the pot, pushed and manoeuvred by his wooden spoon. He loved making jam. It gave him immense satisfaction, second only to the pleasure of eating it.
"Your jam's in the way."
This time he could not ignore the statement as her voice reached a crescendo that jerked him back to reality.
"Pardon ?"
"Your jam's in the way. How many times do I have to tell you?"
He stared at her in disbelief. How could the jam be in the way? There were only four jars left anyway! They only took up a small section of the cupboard. They were the only things in the cupboard that belonged to him anyway. Of course, that was it - something that belonged to him was in the cupboard - in her eyes it had no right to be there.

"Well..."

"Well what?" Jack asked, still keeping calm although he now realised what was to come.
'Well, are you going to move it? It's in the way. I can't do with it there. It will have to go. It's nothing but a nuisance. It's terrible stuff anyway. I don't know what you see in the stuff ..."
On and on and on her voice droned; he switched off audibly but the anger began to rise within him. Here we go again, he thought as he spurred into action.
"Are you listening to me? Why don't you get your ears tested?"
" I've had my ears tested, there's nothing wrong with them."
"There must be; you never listen to me. Now what about this jam? Get it moved. I can't do with it here. It's yours, you move it."
That was enough. Slowly but surely, he put his half eaten sandwich on the plate. He walked over to the cupboard and stretched up to the shelf.

"Don't worry," he said calmly, knowing that his very calmness was more of an irritant than rising to her bait.
"Don't worry- I won't make any more - I'll take it outside and let it get frosted and spoilt."
He walked out of the kitchen door and heard her voice still pounding in his eardrums like the pistons of a well oiled engine. He would have the last word he decided - he would throw in one last quip then close the door quickly to avoid another torrent of insults.
"I must be the only person in England who keeps their jam in the shed."

Katy's Friends

Desirée Fearon

At first glance you may have thought that the two girls noisily getting on the bus were sisters. The same multi-shaded blond hair, same height and build and dressed similarly, but if you had studied their clothes you would have seen that one was better dressed than the other. Both girls wore black leggings but the second girl's were shiny, thin and cheap and she carried a large plastic multi-coloured bag. Her friend had a stout, black, well-worn leather bag draped across her body. She slid gracefully into an empty seat whilst her companion threw herself in next to her, pulling at her bag and clothing before settling down with a sigh.

"Going to Primani?" asks Girl number two. She needs a name; shall we call her Val?

"Not today," her companion answers, "I told you I'm going into 'New College' to see about enrolling."

"Oh, Yeh, ya did. I don't know why ya don't come an' work with me. Money's good! We 'ave a right laugh."
Girl number one, let's call her, Fay, a good old fashioned name. It suits her!
She doesn't answer. She chews at a false fingernail and stares out of the window, hiding her irritation from the other girl. This must have been an old topic, because she doesn't answer.
Val may be aggrieved; she shifts sideways on her seat towards the

isle.

"I hate this bus, it always stinks of fried chicken or somefink, and when we get to West Bridgford it'll fill up dead quick. It is sooo boring. Wish I had a car, I could give you a lift in."

"I didn't know you could drive."

"Well I can't, but if I could I would. Yeah."
Their noisy conversation continues in this way for some time, presenting a stage show for the other passengers, who have nothing else to do, being a captive audience.
A woman on her phone keeps ringing the same number and glancing at the girls as if it is their fault she is getting no response.
 An elderly man rattles his newspaper continuously in protest.
An old lady and a young woman, who don't know each other and are sat on opposite sides, grin at each other and nod, acknowledging their shared sense of fun.
The little green bus trundles on, stops, starts then stops again. People get on. People get off. At Radcliffe on Trent it starts to rain. Big grey clouds roll over the sky, taking the light from the inside of the bus, adding gloom to the gloomy. Some dry people get off to be replaced by wet ones with dripping brollies and soggy bags and squeaky shoes.
The girls chatter on in loud brash voices, although one is louder and sillier than the other. The woman is slapping her naughty phone. The old man is reading his paper upside down, and the two women are lifting their shoulders and hanging their heads with sly glances at each other across the aisle, smiles curving and eyes sparkling. What a joy a sense of humour is!
The bus pulls into Tudor Square in West Bridgford and stops outside 'Iceland'. There are quite a few people getting off and on here. The driver lingers, and as he waits a young couple come into our view, intertwined, and sharing a golfing umbrella. A sudden

gust of wind lifts the front and we see their happy faces. They laugh and he kisses her.
There is a scrabble, a scream, arms and legs flailing. Val tries to push her contorted face to the window.

"Look, look, look," she cries, "It's Carl, Katy's Carl. The little shit!"

"Sit down or get off," shouts the driver.

"Shut up!" Orders the elderly man, crumpling up his newspaper.
I bet he was in the army.

The woman vigorously shakes her phone.
The two women make snorting sounds, their shoulders shake with the mirth of it all, and they look at each other. What fun we are having they seem to say, with their wide eyes and grimaces.
Fay pulls her friend down into her seat.

"Oh, that's his sister. I met her once, she's very nice."
She sounds unconvincing. Is someone telling porkies?
Val is not having any oil poured on her troubled waters.

"No, it's not. Nobody kisses their sister like that. Oh, poor Katy, she'll be devastated. I warned her he was like that. He's a right slag. I'll have to tell her, she's my best mate."
She glowers at Fay, who is definitely not her best mate.

"Think about it," reasons Fay, "you don't know for sure. If you get in the middle, you'll only get the blame. Anyway, I thought you used to fancy him."

"Me? It weren't me. I hate him. Bloody pig!"
The fur flies!

We had best close our ears to the many faults of poor Carl, who has enough of them to carry us to the end of our journey.
The bus reaches the terminus, Friar Lane. Everyone gets off.
The woman has killed her phone and stuffs it into her bag. Serves it right, she thinks.
 The two women get up one after the other, not making eye contact. After all, they were never introduced, and leave the bus silently.
Val takes one last stab at it.

"Everyone on the bus saw him, they could tell her," she sulks.
The elderly man thrusts his newspaper into the bin.

"Fat chance," he says.

I gather my stuff together and get off the bus.
The driver stands up and stretches and then follows.
 "This is what they call fresh air," he says to me.

Blood and Fire

Marie Ng Perez

we had a white christmas in 2010
i remember it all too well
mi mate jim never saw it to the thaw
he were buried in a plain box
6ft below the snow up on wilford hill
a cremation would 'ave been ironic
too late to warm weary bones
by a roaring fire

standing by a hole in the earth
with only a solitary magpie for company
i was, 'the one for sorrow'
later, i'd drown that sorrow
in a bottle of smart price gin
0% temperance in that

jim's whole life came down to
this one paltry box
give all my stuff t'sally
was his last request
but you can keep the empty box
he mocked

three days pissed
three days passed
till i were sober enuff
to take jim's stuff

the box held riches
full of memories
a kaleidoscopic view
of a colourful past
the sum total of jim's wealth
to anyone else it were probably a box full of tat

i took jim's box t'sally
it was gratefully received
then i got the best offer
i'd had in a long time
christmas dinner with
all the trimmings
plus i pulled a cracker
and got to stay the night

guess i needed to be grateful
to general william booth for that

The Kindness of Strangers

Desirée Fearon

The first thing you would have noticed, was the moon. It was big and new-washed and so bright that the sky was almost daylight blue. Thready, off-white clouds flew across it, chased by the last winds of what had been three long days of continuous rain, that had finally ended. The low trees in the woods dripped and sighed. The small creatures stuck their heads out of their dens and sniffed the air for food.
The Woodland Hotel was quiet and the few lights that were burning seemed dimmed by the brightness of the moon. It was very late and so still that you might have thought that no-one was about. But behind the desk, Krum sat bent over an old notebook. He was reading from a computer screen and making notes into the book with a short pencil stub pushed into a cardboard tube.
The pencil had belonged to his grandfather, who had put a few away against the coming of technology, advising him that what went so easily into a machine, could just as easily come out.
Krum wrote, 'only one booking, Mr...' He copied the name laboriously into his book. Ah! 'May be addressed as Fred...' Great! 'Arriving after breakfast'. . Humph!
He'll be cutting it fine, then. Conference starts at nine sharp, tomorrow. 'Is there transport booked?' There is.
Krum was the owner of the hotel, which had sort of grown out of the forest. It was warm and woody, with a single storey, and little passages that led to little secluded places. It served plain but delicious food from all around the galaxy, and would serve it in your room at no extra charge.

In its day, it had been the centre for all the science conferences, but now there were so many that a purpose-built place had been set up over the hill, so now there were far fewer visitors than there had been.

Krum did not mind. He had very little interest in all this science talk. Most of it was well over his head, and anyway, mostly failed to deliver what it promised, and when it did, it wasn't necessarily what you had wanted in the first place.

He raised his tall stooping frame. He hoped he'd get some better sleep tonight, now that the wind was dying down.

"I'll get a drink and go to bed," he said to himself, and turning off the computer, put his notebook in his pocket and shuffled off.

The four-armed chef from Glooop, was just finishing the second serving of breakfast when Mr Fred arrived. Krum booked him in and offered refreshments which he declined, so he popped him into the conference flyer, and sent him off again as swiftly as he had arrived. He said that he would not return until late, but ordered some insect paté and greens, for his return.

Krum was walking in the garden with his wife and child when Mr Fred returned. Mrs Krum took the child inside as Krum greeted him.

"Will you take a drink, sir? The bar is just across from reception. Would you like to eat in there or in your room?"

"In there will be fine, thank you. Do you have Portrian brandy?"

"Yes, indeed. It's very popular here. Have you had a good day?"

"Oh, yes. There are plenty of ideas out there. Making them work is another thing. Hang on... my translator's packing up... Oh, that's better."

Krum poured the drinks.

"Your world's a desert, I believe; we too have desert areas. On the equator, of course."

Mr Fred thought about his home, built into a cave in the dusty, red desert, and of the small tree that died because he just couldn't keep it moist enough. He thought of Karmel who had died of fever in

her mother's arms, and of Willa who had died of grief soon after.
He thought how he had quit the place. Brushed off the dust for ever. Thoughtfully he answered Krum's implied question.
"Yes, but that wasn't always the case. Same old, same old. Too many people, too few resources left. Not enough water to go around anymore. Of course, we thought there would always be answers. Big mistake. I spend most of my time travelling from world to world, trying to come up with some solutions."
"And have you found any here?"
Mr Fred's meal had arrived. He started to pick at it.
"If you think going into the asteroid belt and lassoing an ice meteorite and towing it back, is some sort of solution."
He laughed, but his eyes held a sad sort of heaviness, like a man who knew he wasn't making any difference...
He picked up the breakfast menu.
"Foods of the worlds," he read. "I quite like otherworld foods. Oh, I don't know – I have to leave early tomorrow. I'm booked on the flyer to Blunto. I'll try your English breakfast. In my room, if that's OK."
"You're a man on the move. Yes, happy to help."
Krum was glad he was Krum and not one of these sad men who wandered the Universe, looking for immortal worlds. Did they not realise that we all live on lumps of rock hurtling through space, going nowhere, with no purpose? He reached out and sort of touched Mr Fred.
"You should get yourself a wife and family. No point in making yourself miserable for the rest of your life."
Mr Fred pushed his plate aside and smiled wryly at Krum.
"Well, that's me for the night. See you in the morning." And he dragged himself off to his room.
Next morning, Mr Fred and Krum stood outside the hotel waiting for the balloon taxi to the space dome to arrive.
Mr Fred looked at the woods still dripping with the rain. His foot felt wet. He looked down to find he was standing in a puddle. He

hadn't known that his shoes let in water. He took in the blue, blue sky, the green of the grass and trees; the cool peace of the entire place.

He raised his arm, sweeping it into a large arc encompassing the scene.

"Be careful, Mr Krum," he said, "I must warn you that Earth, my Earth, was once like this..."

♦♦♦

The Red Dress

Ann Packwood

"A lady in a long red dress has been following us. Who is she?" enquired one of the gentlemen in the party of ex Naval Officers being shown around Exton Castle.

"I'm sorry, I don't know who you are talking about, I haven't seen a lady in a long red dress," answered the tour guide.

As a guide for the Duke of Exton, she had seen many things and been asked many questions, but never one about a lady in a long red dress. In any case, all the tour guides and wardens were under strict instructions not to talk about ghosts in the Castle to any of the visitors.

She quickly ushered the party into the next room and began pointing out the different pieces of antique furniture, relaying the history of the castle and the portraits of the Earls and Dukes of Exton hanging on the wall. All were resplendent in their Garter Robes of red capes edged with ermine over doublet and hose, their feet encased in black shoes with a silver buckle on the front. They all had a haughty expression on their face.

"Don't take any notice of him," one of the women in the party sidled up to her and whispered. "He's drunk!"

Indeed the party had enjoyed a lunch in the castle restaurant before the tour, but the gentleman in question didn't appear to be drunk, just bewildered, as he kept looking around as if expecting to find someone standing beside him. Nothing more was said about the lady in red.

When the tour ended, and before going into the Warden's room for a welcome cup of tea, the guide took a walk back along the route of the tour. Reaching the corridor which led to the Long Gallery she stood looking at one of the portraits. It was labelled 'Frances, daughter of the 6th Earl of Exton'. It was a full-length portrait of Frances dressed in the fashion of the day. The artist must have been exceptionally gifted as he had captured the essence of the lady, hair neatly arranged off her face, her fine features, clear blue eyes looking directly at you and a demure smile on her lips.

The opulence of her dress was there for all to see, its richness, the vibrant red colour, and the intricate delicate lace pattern of her v shaped collar showing off the creamy white skin of her neck.

As the guide moved away from the portrait she caught a flash of red out of the corner of her eye.

Until she started to work at Exton Castle she didn't believe in ghosts. That was until she saw the lady in the portrait, the lady in the long red dress, walk down the corridor and disappear through the wall into the Dining Room.

Resistance is fertile

Maria Ng Perez

sex used to be fun

but it's turned into a chore

done with strategic military precision

there's no pleasure in it any more

Private Johnson's ordered to stand to attention

the wife chills my boxers in the fridge

that's a form of corporal punishment

Private Johnson's gone AWOL and hid

it has to be against the Geneva Convention

it's inhumane that I'm shrivelled, blue and sore

I'm sure my bits have frost bite

it's so hard

it needs to thaw

anytime of the day or night

I could get a poke in the ribs

don't get me wrong

I believe in free love 'n' liberty

but I never signed up for this

I think I've run out of ammunition

I'm sure I'm firing blanks

I shot my load three times last night

and I didn't even get a thanks!

I've been banned from drinking alcohol

I'm not allowed to smoke

this trying for a baby malarkey

has turned my life into a joke

but then she came out of the bathroom

and showed me a solid line of blue

then I realised I hadn't really minded doing

every single thing she asked me to

Up a Gum Tree

Desiree Fearon

As the train gathered speed I suddenly realised that I had left the chewing-gum stuck onto the top of the chocolate biscuit. There it was, I hadn't even given it another thought. My mother had told me my slovenly ways would be my undoing, huh! The old bag was probably right.
I found a fresh pack of gum in my pocket. Not that it was my fault really, I mean to say if it hadn't have been for that ugly cow next door to Nan none of it would have happened, it was all her fault. Every time I went around there she'd rush out of her front door with some tale or other about who had called on the old girl, how long they stayed, you know the drill.
Smoked like a chimney she did - we had that much in common. That's why it was her fault, you see.
One day I made my mind up "No more fags" I said to myself, and I meant it, like that I am, makes up my mind. That's it. Job done.

So that day, I goes round to see the old girl, cadge a few bob, you know, Ugly comes out, giving it this, 'Yak-Yak.' Well I'd got the best part of a pack of fags in my pocket so I bunged 'em to her. I'm kind like that y'know. Talk about grovel, it was an embarrassment. But she tells me all sorts of things about the old girl I didn't know before. Later I bought some more fags and collected some empty packets off the street and sort of shared them out, you know, a couple or so per pack to keep 'Old Ugly' sweet, you know the drill. Trouble was, because I had the fags hanging around so as to speak, I was gasping! So I started buying that special chewing gum, but here I was off the fags but addicted to the gum!

Of course, it was all the old girls fault really, I mean to say, we didn't always get on, she was prim and proper 'old school', and I couldn't give a monkeys. So it was often, like, "why d'you dress like that, or you wasn't brought up to swear, or drop your aitches," or some such crap. But I was her only relation so I had to keep an eye on 'er money. I mean she might have given it to anyone. Right?

I goes round there, Tuesday it was, always Tuesday, nothing on the telly. Same time, same place. Well she got the 'ump with me, all over them ruddy biscuits. She always got them same ones from this posh shop, up town, ever since I was a kid, big ones, hand dipped in chocolate, but I was only ever allowed one you see. So I used to riffle though them for the one with the most chocolate on it, sort of got to be a habit, like. She'd lay them out all neat in this silver dish, many a time I got a clip round the ear for messing them up, I can tell you.

Well I was shuffling through them that day when she says.
"Do you have to do that, you're not a child anymore, why are you so greedy?"

Well I didn't want to start her off did I? So I changed the subject.

"Nan" I said "Can you lend me a fiver, I'm spent up till Friday."

She gave me a queer look " How's that? I thought you'd be a lot better off now you're not smoking. And since when have I lent you money, I can't remember a time you ever paid me back."

"Come off it, 'course I don't, you're my Nan."
Silly old bag! Then she says, all prim like.

"I don't have any, anyway. I haven't been to the cash point this week. It's been too cold to go out, and I'm OK till the end of the week."

LIAR! LIAR! Pants on fire! Before I come in I'd been talking to Ugly, and she had told me they'd been into town on the bus the day before. She'd picked up her money, and done some shopping. And that wasn't all she told me and I'll tell you, I was not best pleased.

Apparently, they'd only decided to go on holiday, to some posh hotel together, and I could guess who was paying for that since it was obvious Ugly didn't have a pot to pee in.

Anyway I waited till Nan went to the lavvy and dipped into her purse, she must have had about seventy pounds there, so I helped myself to a twenty, just to learn her, and went home.

Well the next Tuesday, I got off the bus and there was Ugly waiting for me, I thought the 'Old Girl' must've popped her clogs and I was feeling quite chirpy, but no. 'Ugly' grabs my arm and asks me if I had brought anything for Nan. Well no, 'course I hadn't, never brought her nothing did I, 'cept maybe Christmas, Smellies, Chocolates or an ornament from the charity shop. Well crumblies like them things don't they?

Well she sets about me something fierce, said the Old Girl told her I was stealing money off her. Well I put on my aggrieved face, and said she give it me and must have forgot. But the next thing was worse. Ugly said that the Old Girl wanted her to go to a solicitor with her so she could make a will out. I said what did she want to do that for. There's only me, family.

Ugly said that the old bugger was going to leave her, Ugly, one thousand pounds and the rest to Green Peace. Green Peace! I ask you. There was the shop she rents out, half a dozen houses - and my flat. Oh, my good night, I'd have to start paying rent! Over her dead body!
That was when I made my mind up. Again. I went to Nans'. She was a bit frosty, and for once I tried to be nice, but I ended up not stopping long. She didn't mention it and I didn't ask, so there wasn't much to say really, though I did manage to nick her key. That didn't matter, I intended to return it on my next visit and she had several, she was always losing them anyway.

The next day I went to the bus station and caught a bus to the next town. I went to B & Q and bought a pair of loose overalls and some disposable gloves, and then I went to a charity shop and bought some shoes, two sizes too big. I managed to pull an old piece of rope out of a skip on the way back to the bus station; I was well pleased with myself.

It was a 'orrible bad night, raining and that, just as well really. I let myself into her house, she was in bed asleep. It didn't take long, she was frail and I was determined.

Afterwards I messed the place up, took some money and valuables, walked all over the house in them big shoes... I intended to take them back to the next town A.S.A.P. and dump them in a building skip.
I thought, as the holiday was booked I might as well take it. Just to look good I'd take Ugly too. She was well cut up about the old girl, funny that, kept crying. I thought she's was gonna be a barrel of laughs.
But I never found out.

Trouble was I couldn't resist them biscuits so I grabbed the best one, but you can't eat biscuits and chew gum at the same time can you.
So I shoved the gum into the dish.

That's how they got my DNA.

If I Ruled the World

Roger Smith

…dry discussions like this would not 'cut it'. One needs charisma!

It seems to me that 'If I Ruled the World' is an extreme form of

'If it were up to me…'

Which may have progressed through

'If I were in charge…'

to

'If I were in the Prime Ministers shoes…'

with

'If I ruled the world…'

being the ultimate statement used

by those exasperated governments who do not seem to have a clue.

I am told that everyone says such things, yet what are we really talking about?

Has anyone ever ruled the world? Could anyone ever rule the world?

I am told that everyone says this sort of thing, but what are we talking about?

Alexander the Great, Julius Caesar, Genghis Khan, Napoleon and Hitler, all seemed to be intent on ruling very large chunks of the world. Beyond killing people and having a lot of people working on some big projects, their power was very much limited by the majority who did not want to be ruled by them.

Let us forget any military take over. Perhaps in a more ideal world, the appointed Secretary General of the United Nations could be the top person and have the mandate to say what is best for the world.

Might it be better to elect a leader than appoint one? I have never stood for election
and am not able to imagine being elected leader of the UN, so how about a lottery to decide who will be the ruler of the world?
Maybe this is not so crazy in these days of an annual crowning of a 'King or Queen of the Jungle' based on a TV show and a phone in. Taking this popular concept further, it does not have to be a game show, just a way of using technology to give any celebrity or better still, any ordinary person the very top job for a set period.

Now I have proposed a vague idea of how I could, with a one in seven billion chance, become a popular leader of the world. What on earth would I do with this opportunity?

For starters, it is not just what on Earth. There would be nothing to stop me from **asking nations** to unite in a serious effort to colonise Mars. Before talking more about policy that last sentence contains the words 'asking' and 'nations' which I believe reveals the most important things to know about ruling the world.

Firstly about **Asking:** As ruler of the world one would surely be able to say, 'this is what we are going to do'… although that brings Flash Gordon's foe, Ming the Merciless to mind. To have everyone obey is either going to take a lot of fear, or some kind of mind control? We might just as well have Alexander the Great in charge! He was not great, in my opinion, as much of his power was derived from massacring civilians. I think it is healthy to be a leader of the world, rather than a ruler.

Nations? I said 'nations' I am imagining one becoming leader of the world we live in today, with 200+ nations and each nation having their own leader(s) I am imagining the new world leader's task will be to lead the leaders. Doing that would be great, but would fail to please billions as so many leaders are failing to do what their people want. Surely it is these leaders **not** doing what we hope for them to do that leads to us saying, 'If I were in charge…'

I believe the new leader, me or you, would need to be able to talk directly to leaders of many organisations and even to individuals, as well as to the leaders of nations.

You or I would need some clear policies. What would you or I want to change first?

Whether organising our personal life or a whole planet, we still have to choose between prioritising on urgency or importance. Politicians know their time in power is limited, and so tend to be driven by urgency. They have pressures such as balancing the economy right now. These pressures make many of their dreams beyond them, as their term in office comes to an end too soon.

Ultimate power gives one the choice to be different, but what a choice.

Being in a position to talk to all sides in the Syrian conflict and perhaps end the war by Christmas - yes, this Christmas – now that has got to be urgent and I could imagine would please almost everyone on Earth to see the inhabitants of Aleppo not killing but rebuilding.

Sadly, I believe a horrible truth is that on a world wide scale Syria and Aleppo are not that important. Yes, any leader of the world is going to be called callous from time to time as tough decisions are going to be needed.

When 'important' does not have to be 'urgent' a leader may have more options.

So, my first policy, and my first meeting? What I have in mind is not going to get me elected and right now would not even be that popular.

Since looking in my parents huge Readers Digest Atlas of the World at the age of six, I have known without a shadow of doubt the biggest problem the world has to face up to. It is a mathematical thing that is an inescapable truth. The graph in the atlas showed the exponential rise in world population. Fifty two years later the predicted increase has occurred along with all the problems predicted from rising populations. There are simply more and more people in a world with less and less resources.

My first meetings will be with the religious leaders asking they reconsider policies regarding contraception. I would take that 1960's atlas as well as using sophisticated presentation aids to explain how suffering, including civil wars are largely driven by too many people with seemingly too little to go around.

As for Syria? The statistics are available on line. The country's population increased faster than almost any country ever in the years leading up to the civil war. There were millions of babies born into a country unable to cope with such a population explosion. Okay, So things are never as simple as one change causes a war, or one change solves everything. I just felt I needed to share that if you want to be a leader of the world or a responsible Ruler of the World then everything will hinge on you abilities to:
a) grasp the bigger picture.
b) Persuade those who most need to be persuaded.

You will also need to bear in mind that no matter how popular you or I are on day one, the chances are that a lot of people are going to be disappointed no matter what you do.

A smattering of life or death.

Brenda Dobson   A villanelle Winter 2016

1. The scent of death comes with the wind

'I lift my eyes to the hills', 'I chose to climb'

Lifelong dreams, face the bitter end.

2. No belief in God, he prayed as if he had sinned,

Frozen fingers, skeleton white, broken limbs

The scent of death, comes with the wind.

3. Broken beard, broken heart, broken mind

Between half lives, the snowy blanket insulates him.

Lifelong dreams, face the bitter end.

4. Hopes of finding him alive are slim.

Some found, the searching comes to an end

The scent of death comes with the wind.

5. White scars, blood drained

The scent of death comes with the wind

Lifelong dreams face the bitter end.

Mrs Hardcastle and the Board of Mothers

Jan Parnham

Sophie had recently moved into the small village, ten miles out from Sheffield with her husband and two young children, Kerry, aged eight, and Michael, six. The children had started at the local school where Sophie would take them and pick them up after school. She would stand alone, as she was rather shy. She was attractive in a natural way, with fair skin and mid length wavy blonde hair. Sophie wore rather simple clothes, slightly ethnic in style, and had moved up from the South of England, where she had grown up. The other mothers seemed to ignore her, although she always said 'Hello' and gave them a genuine kind smile. She was becoming desperate to be accepted in the village and very much wished to join in the community activities, but most of the inhabitants kept her at a distance as she was not a local from the area and spoke with an odd accent.

One morning while she was shopping at the village store, she spotted a notice asking for helpers to produce cakes for the Spring Fair stall, which would be in five weeks time. So off Sophie went to the local village hall for the meeting to discuss the forthcoming fair. As she walked in there were most of the mothers she saw regularly at the gates, chatting away, laughing, and getting very involved with plans for the coming event. Mrs Elizabeth Hardcastle, who appeared to be in charge, was issuing out the list of cakes to each mother to supply with quantity and sizes she required. Sophie thought she must have been in the army, as they seemed too like orders, rather than requests. Finally, Mrs Hardcastle (her name suited her) noticed Sophie, she said, 'Are you here to help then?' in a matter of fact way. Sophie nodded, so was given the order to supply one simple Victoria sponge with jam and fresh cream to make for the next meeting, so it could be tasted and see if it was good enough. Sophie was a little taken aback, but accepted the challenge. It might enable her to become one of the accepted ones, as that seemed to be what was expected.

In the next week she made three sponges, which were getting better as she was still trying to get used to her oven which was electric; previously, she had always cooked with gas, it did seem to make a big difference. She had to admit the first sponge was a disaster although her children were happy to eat it.
The day arrived for her to take her sample sponge for test marketing by Mrs Hardcastle and her board (so it seemed) of obedient mothers. The sponge rose beautifully, she used her own home made raspberry jam and whipped up fresh double cream, sandwiched it together and sprinkled icing sugar on top. She was extremely pleased with her work. The telephone rang so she popped into the hall to answer it. When she returned to the kitchen she was horrified to see that the cake had been sabotaged – by her cat who was happily sitting on the table, cleaning his paws from all the that delicious cream he managed to lick and scrape from the cake.

Sophie cried, and after screaming at the cat, sat down feeling very lonely and unhappy. Suddenly she got up , said to herself 'you have two hours before the testing, pull yourself together and get on with the task in hand'.

She worked fast and produced yet another good looking sponge, this time she put it into a tin for safety. She had a quick cup of tea, then set off to see the masters of the cake stall. She entered the hall, went over to the table where Mrs Hardcastle was, took out her sponge and placed it on a very pretty cake stand that she had, of course, brought with her, smiled, and stood back in anticipation.

The sponge was scrutinised from every angle, then cut into eight pieces and given out to the 'board of mothers'. Sophie waited, the silence was haunting, then suddenly, the verdict. Mrs Hardcastle looked up, a gradual smile appeared, and finally she said it was delicious, light, nice colour, lovely jam and just the right amount of cream. The board of mothers, of course, all agreed, nodded and finally started to communicate with Sophie – apparently the ice had melted; their mentor, Mrs Hardcastle, had given her approval.

So Sophie had been accepted at school, she was welcomed into the morning and afternoon chatter with the mums. When the Fair arrived, Sophie took her sponges to the cake stall and helped to sell them, and that's how she finally received the friendship and loyalty of the mothers of the village. Just shows what a Victoria sponge can do.

Rescue Mission.

Maud Harris

"For you, soldier, the sands of time just ran out."

Crouching on the straw covered floor of a damp cell, the lone window high up beyond his reach letting in a murky light and no warmth, Jed looked at his captor. After three months of captivity, fed on watery soup and rice, he didn't much care either way as long as it was quick. Even the all pervading stench of mould and urine no longer bothered him.
Hassan, the guard, disappointed at not getting the reaction he wanted, tried a different approach.

"The penalty for spying is execution," his bloodshot brown eyes bored into Jed. "They will come for you at dawn, you will be led out to the courtyard where you will be shot. Your body will be fed to the dogs after the women have finished with it."

Hassan took pleasure in taunting his prisoners; the threat of execution was a common one. The first time, Jed had been terrified as he was shackled, blindfolded and led into the courtyard and forced to kneel in the dust. Not much of a one for religion, he had prayed that day. The seething anger that he felt when his captors roughly pulled his chains and marched him back to the cell never left him. The mixed feelings of relief, humiliation and fear left him trembling.
   The spy drone beamed back images of the clearing adjacent to the pass. At first the pictures were of the Hindu Kush mountains

with no special features, but when co-ordinated they showed a pattern. Expert camouflage concealed a rocky courtyard where sentries patrolled. Three heavily camouflaged gun emplacements were carefully hidden amid the rough terrain. The images were immediately wired through to the base at Credenhill in Herefordshire.

A meeting was underway; Sgt Geordie McAndrews briefed his team. Chuck Peters, a rangy, loose limbed man of about thirty, Chuck should have been a sergeant by now. His service record was exemplary – or it had been until he had disobeyed a direct order. The mission had been to rescue the kidnapped daughter of a prominent government official. The child was saved, but Chuck narrowly escaped with his life. He was lucky to escape a court martial, and was demoted a rank. This was to be his first mission since that debacle.
Private Rod Simmons was fairly new to the SAS, he had been with 1 Para before selection. Jerry Tweedy comprised the fourth member of the team, a good man to have at your back, but his problems with aggression sometimes affected his judgement.

"As you know," Geordie began. "All our missions carry an element of danger, and this one is no different. This mountain terrain does us no favours; the target is one of our own. Some of you will know Jed Lacey."

"Oh shit! The poor bastard" interjected Jerry. Those ragheads don't muck about"

"He's been held hostage for the last three months. HQ think they have identified the camp, so, come on lads, let's go get him."

Under cover of darkness the Chinook helicopter hovered as, one by one the team parachuted out, their balaclavas and black jump suits rendered them almost invisible. The chopper sped away, leaving

them with their heavy backpacks, climbing gear and rifles. Huddling in the shelter of a rock by torchlight, Geordie surveyed the map.
"We'll make our way to this point,"
He indicated a spot on the map overlooking the camp.
"Then we hole up while daylight lasts. We mount a surprise attack at midnight. And remember, guys, a quick in and out is what we're looking at. We don't know what state Jed will be in, so be prepared."

Hassan and his rebel colleagues were sleeping off the effects of rough alcohol and drugs when the SAS team reached the compound. The lone guard, snapping awake half a minute too late, was overpowered from behind and silenced by Jerry's blade cutting through his jugular before he could raise the alarm. Withdrawing a bolt cutters from his backpack, Rod cut through the chain securing the rickety door.
Jed stared in disbelief as Rod burst into the cell; it took just a few seconds for him to realise what was happening.
"You OK?"

"Yeah! Get me out of here, like NOW!"

Chuck had radioed ahead for the helicopter, and as the five of them made their way stealthily across the courtyard, keeping to the shadows, Hassan, awakened from a drunken stupor by some instinct, approached the cell with his machete at the ready. He found himself face to face with Jerry. As their eyes met Jerry levelled his Glock pistol. Just before his head exploded, Hassan was aware, with brutal clarity, for him, the sands of time had run out.

Tree of Life

Jan Parnham

The seed is sown from whence it drops
Is covered with the life of past
Down trodden by the passing life
To start a future of thine own

The seed it sprouts beneath the earth
Its shoots stretch out within the sod
And given time a tender branch reaches for the light
Bursting forth towards the light so strong
Its tender fragile frame emerges from the depths
To see a bright new world above a hidden mother earth
Mother Nature tends her young, to grow from strength to strength
The little shoot from tender earth shoots forth towards a tree

Through many seasons of weather varied
The tree learns of its nature, from within
It grows, it forms, it stretches forth
To stand among the tallest

Its arms outstretched with leaves of many
Its flowers, its sap, its strength of being
Supports the forthcoming of its brothers
From natures loved and varied forms

Coming from earth the insects many
Encroach upon the branches, reaching forth to light
The winged flights of birds find refuge there
Amongst the branches deep
The sound of birds chatter, song and flight
The whisper of the wind amongst the leaves

The rain doth fall as scattered food
The wind blows dust and earth away
The sun brings strength and light so strong to stay
To house the inhabitants of life, amongst the tree

The animals, both man and mammal
Shelter from the storm, rest and grow
From whence the air is freshened
For life seen, unseen, emerges from the tree

And grows from strength to strength
From branches stretching from all sides
A canopy of life
The tree has grown from strength to strength
From a seed of love and light

Confusion

Desiree Fearon

I was half way out of the taxi when my shoe dropped off. I had to step onto the wet pavement to retrieve it, only to find that the sole was flapping in the wind, so as to speak. I tried to put it on anyway, but on walking it flopped down and dragged along the pavement. As if this wasn't bad enough I had arrived already late at my destination, where I was to be the guest of honour. It was pouring with rain, so no one was there to greet me. I turned to get back into the taxi, but I was too late, it was already driving away. I was just recovered from two weeks in bed with the flu. This was all I needed.

Now as guest of honour, in some countries, I would have been greeted and fussed over, someone dispatched to find me alternative shoes, probably dried off, and made to feel good about myself again, but this is England. Go barefoot or not at all. Oliver Cromwell and the puritans have a lot to answer for. As it was, I stood about for a few moments waiting for someone, anyone, to appear. It soon became apparent that nobody was coming. I was, as they say, flying solo.

I went into the Assembly Rooms, very Jane Austin, complete with authentic dust, economy lighting, and a cracked tiled floor. If I had two good shoes I would have been tempted to waltz across the floor in the imaginary arms of some handsome and superior young officer, yes, I know they didn't waltz in those days but it's my fantasy and I'll do what I want. I squelched across to the set of doors nearest me, opened one and peered in, in the glow from the reception room all I could see in there were a few gilt chairs stacked higgledy- piggledy. No-one in there then. Try the next door.

Oooh-er, isn't this exciting – not. What do we have here? A clean white board, some tables and plain plastic chairs, and incongruously a teddy bear on the floor just inside the door. One more set of doors on this side and then the grand staircase. Of course in the more civilised parts of the country, and America they have boards up in the entrance. Blue Room – Dental Conference, Red Room – Cooking for Goldfish. Gents Toilets to the left. Ladies Powder Room three floors up. But not here. Enter at your peril, here.

Only one door this time and locked, what is in there then, I must know. LET ME IN! Alright then don't, see if I care. Should I go up the stairs or leave that adventure till last. Well if I walk up I may have to walk all the way down again to no good purpose, so I'll leave it for now. Gosh these stairs are wide. Next little door, cloakroom. Rails and hangers. No coats! No coats. Strange. Not a Mac' not an umbrella or a pair of wellies. Zilch, Nada, Nowt.

Hey! No noise, no laughing, no music, no drunks. No nothing. Am I here…Yes, I'm here, thank heavens for that. Perhaps I've moved into parallel universe. Died, Oh Shoot! Have I got the wrong night? All this dressing up, coming out in the rain. Losing my shoe. All for nothing. Walking on deeper into the building, behind a set of dusty green velvet curtains half concealing a door marked 'No Entry', I eventually found a cleaning lady who let me use the phone and I rang for another taxi. I ran out barefoot into the rain and climbed in. The taxi driver stared at me. "I hope you haven't got my carpets wet." He said.

Phil Atelist

Maria Ng Perez

Phil was a collector of stamps. From his youth to becoming a man, it still remained his no.1 passion. He cherished each small and delicate masterpiece.

On the surface, Ms Penelope Noir was a rare beauty, but you didn't need a magnifying glass to see that her looks were only paper thin. She was jagged round the edges, not a first class type but Ms Noir believed that she was the real deal and that Phil was lucky to have her as his prized possession.

Penelope delivered Phil her ultimatum;

'If you really loved me
You'd sell those stamps' she sobbed
'It's you that should be paying
For my boob job
Don't you think it's time
You swapped your boyhood passion?
Maybe you'd show me some consideration
If I put sex
On stamp rations
Am I not more of a desirable mount than they?
Just list them all
And get shot
Of the lot

On eBay
The time has come
For you to choose'
She felt confident
That Phil would prefer
Her as his muse

Silently, Phil contemplated for a few moments, before closing his stamp album, tucking it under his arm and walking out the door, shutting it firmly behind him. It hadn't taken him long to come to the conclusion, that he was better off waiting for his genuine Penny Black, rather than settling for any fakes.

The Egg

Jan Parnham

Betty and Grace were great friends, they did everything together, any spare time they had, one would see them, laughing, running and playing all around the village. They were inseparable. Both girls had grown up in the small village, a few miles out of Cambridge; both girls were only children of poor families who had managed to survive through the Second World War. Both fathers had fought and had sustained injuries. Money was short, so Betty and Grace were dressed in rather old and worn second hand clothes. They had long hair which was plaited, only one pair of shoes and one coat each, which was a little larger so that they could grow into it. They had enough fresh vegetables, which their mums grew in the small gardens, plus a lot of rabbit stew; the rabbits were caught locally in the countryside by friends and neighbours, who regularly went rabbiting to survive the war and afterwards, enabling them to have fresh meat on the table.

Life for the girls was an adventure, they were quite free to please themselves as long as they were both home by dark, and certainly by dinnertime. They went to the local village school, which only had two teachers; sixteen children attended between five and eleven years old. Betty and Grace were eight, with only two days between their birthdays in June

On one of their days off school, they decided to pack up a sandwich with some tinned spam, a scone each, which Bettys' mum had made, and some water. They set off to explore for the day. There was a large old house, only a couple of miles from the village, which had been bombed during the war, so they were ready to explore the grounds and what remained of the house.

As they neared the building they could see a lot of the front of the house which was still standing, although it appeared very dilapidated. There was wire round part of the building with signs saying 'Danger. Keep Out'. The girls had seen it before, but had never ventured past. But today was different. They managed to get over the wire, which had been pushed down by previous adventurers. They ran over the open ground and went through what would have been a large front door, except, no door, only a grand surround into a fairly large room with no ceiling and rubble everywhere. A few pieces of badly burned furniture, bricks, and broken glass lay around. A fire place only half standing, walls crumbling and a few remaining steps of a grand staircase, which to the girls was as wide as their largest room at home. Grace said "it must have been a very grand building, perhaps a princess lived here. I can see her walking down the staircase in a wonderful long gown with flowers in her hair, with sparkling jewels and her Prince Charming waiting for her at the bottom." Betty smiled. "You have read too many fairy stories, but I must admit, somebody very wealthy must have lived here a long time ago."
They both carried on through the hall to yet another doorless room which seemed enormous. Again no ceiling, only a lovely blue sky. The floor was knee deep in brick rubble, roofing material and timber, much of which had been burnt from the bomb explosion.

Betty and Grace scrambled over the rubble towards what would have been large doors leading on to the terrace, then into a garden. It must have been magnificent in its day, but now basically an empty shell with the rear of the building totally flattened. They both found an old large piece of timber to sit on and have their picnic, being able to look out of the building on to an overgrown garden with large trees to the rear.

As they were eating their lunch, Betty spotted a small glimmer of something shiny in the rubble beneath her foot. She pushed away some of the rubble and found a small egg shaped item covered in grime, dust and vegetation which had started growing in the room. It appeared to be an egg, but was much heavier, hard, and had lots of what appeared to be some type of decoration. This was what had caught Betty's eye, it was shining and she rubbed it with her handkerchief, but the dirt was fixed hard on it. She put it in her pocket to take home and clean it up.

Betty and Grace finished their lunch and carried on exploring what remained of the building, then across the grounds, finding what would have been an enormous conservatory, then lots of broken down outbuildings, possibly stables, green houses and a gazebo. These were all overgrown with vegetation and crumbling bricks. As it was now getting late and they had a couple of miles to walk home they decided to set off after an adventurous day which they had both enjoyed.

On reaching their village they said farewell and went to their separate homes till school the next day. Betty secretively cleaned her egg – it took a long time, she had soaked it in warm soapy water for over an hour, then dried and polished it. It was much prettier than she had imagined, with lots of decoration in relief, in bright colours and it sparkled in parts. She would take it to school and show it to her favourite teacher who liked arty things. Next morning she went off to school, met up with Grace on the way, and showed her the egg. She thought it was wonderful and said it must have been her Princess's.

At break time Betty and Grace saw Miss Tomlinson and showed

her the egg they had found in the ruins. Miss Tomlinson was absolutely amazed; she studied it and found a mark on the underside. It said FABERGE. Later they found out it was gold, embellished with beautiful coloured enamels and jewels. It would have been owned by a wealthy aristocrat, or even royalty.

Alf

Desiree Fearon

Alf saw the last cleaner off the premises and locked up the old red brick school building for the week-end. He got on his ancient, battered bike and rode through the rain the short distance to his small neat terraced house that backed onto the railway line. When he got home he parked his bike in the back yard and covered up the saddle with a Morrison's carrier bag, unlocked the back door and sat on the stoop to remove his boots and old mac. He carried his boots into the dim kitchen and switched on the single pendant light that hung over the sink by the window. Alf got out his boot cleaning kit. He took a pride in his well mended boots; his mother had always said that you could judge a man from the state of his boots. He went back to the stoop and began to clean them.

Alf loved his little two bed-roomed home; it was where he had lived all of his life. He and Charlie had been born there. Strictly speaking, only half the house belonged to him, as it was left to them both, but his brother had told him it was his for life. After Charlie married, the happy couple went to live in a large house up near the golf course. Their Mother hadn't liked Charlie's wife, she said that she was above herself. Mother had been full of rage when Ava had persuaded Charlie to study for an electrician's course and move away from home, even though there wouldn't have been room for them all in the tiny turn of the century house.

Alf put his clean and shiny boots by the back door, washed his hands at the pot sink and switched on the chipped enamel oven. He got a "Pukka-Pie" from the fridge, and popped it into a tin dish. Ten minutes to heat the oven first, mother had said. She had always wanted him to bring fish and chips on a Friday, but Alf had preferred a pie, he fetched a plate from the old painted dresser and laid himself a place at the table. Alf looked at the plastic tablecloth and ill matching cutlery he had inherited, and all the odd plates, years ago he had intended to buy some nice matching ones but mother said it was a waste of money. Ava and Charlie had bought lots when they married and their table had always looked so smart, with warm glowing candles and pretty small flowers, He really enjoyed it when he was asked to eat with them. In the early days of their marriage he had been a frequent visitor and Ava had always made him welcome but after father died, mother didn't like to be left alone for too long, so he couldn't go anymore and eventually the invitations stopped coming.

Alf sat down on the old deal chair that his father used to sit in, and ran his hands over his thinning hair. How mother had hated Ava's golden curls. "Permed and bleached" she said when Charlie had first brought her home. "What the Good Lord gave her not good enough for her, I suppose!"

Alf would have liked to have been married and had a family, it didn't seem right being on his own now, no point to anything really. He put the pie in the oven to warm through, ten minutes at one-fifty degrees. He went through to the living- room and switched on the television to warm up, not that it needed warming up; it was just a habit from the old days. He would eat his pie and then watch the news.
Alf took off his overalls and hung them on a hook in the coat cupboard; he mustn't sit down to tea in his scruff, as mother would have said. He checked his face in the small plastic framed mirror that hung on the back of the cupboard door, the grey gaunt face of an ageing thin man looked back at him. A man alone. Yes, it would have been nice to have someone, if only to moan at him. He had hoped – once.

Mrs Forster had lived next door for years and when her husband died she had thought about moving to small flat, but at that time her niece had been divorced and came to live with her, having no place to go. Her name was Alice and she was a kind, quiet sort of a person and having no training to speak of she took a part-time job in a local shop and then some shifts in the local pub at week-ends. She settled in very well, people liked her, although there was some speculation, and Alf's mother was not slow to add her own penny's-worth.

Alice's day job was at the shop where Alf bought his newspaper, so that was where he first met her. Later he started to call in at the pub for a quick half of 'shandy'. They got on very well and grew closer although they were both very shy. One day Alice came round to Alf's' to help his mother when the wash- boiler broke, she took the linen to the launderette for her, and then persuaded Alf to buy his mother an automatic washing machine. She became flavour of the month with his mother and everything was fine until Alice started talking about going to Australia for a fresh start. Alf and Alice had been courting for some time, and his mother had been alright with that, but she didn't want Alf to go away, they tried to convince her that they would send for her as soon as possible but she didn't like it one bit.

Alf ate his pie, washed up, tidied the kitchen, and moved into the dark beige and brown living-room with the dusty faded wallpaper that he had always meant to decorate, but never got around to. The room was just how his mother had left it with old photos on the sideboard and yellowing lace doilies; long dead dried flowers in a tall vase by the piano and a basket for some unremembered pet. He switched on the electric fire and settled into a shabby velour armchair. He half-heartedly watched the news, but as always, his mind went back to happier days. He picked at the bobbles on his worn brown trousers and thought of the two women in his life, how different they were and how happy they all had become. Their plans for going to Australia nearly finalised until the Asian 'Flu struck. Tomorrow he would take flowers as usual, to both their graves.

My very own place

Brenda Dobson

I've lived here for too many years. My sight is failing. I can't walk down the garden any more, but I still feel as if I am in there, in my own very special place. Trapped in my house, I treasure the memories even more. I see the octagonal shaped terracotta frame, with six windows with a leaded effect. Octagonal shapes lead to a dome on top. The double door at the front opens into an octagonal room with eight chairs set round and octagonal table. I was very pleased with this effect when I first set it up. I could play games of cards with my friends and family. It was romantically lit with candles hanging from the ceiling. The tea lights reflected round the glass walls made it magical. My very own Diwali.
The tea house soon became adopted by my husband and his friends who lived nearby. They would head down the garden of an evening rather than go to the pub.. There they would solve the problems of the universe and education. Naturally the men had to put electricity in, but I still preferred to use candle light. As our children reached their teens, it was their turn to make use of it. My daughter did all her exam revision in it. She could recite out loud to herself without a care in the world; be distracted by the birds and the bees, and the sunshine. She clearly enjoyed being there as she went back for more.

Then the Sixth formers came round. 'Mum, can we go down to the tea house? It's cheaper than going to town.' This was followed by University friends. They all seemed to love it. It allowed them all to make themselves at home, without displacing the parents. It was the place to stay late after the early evening barbecue. They would remain there until the early hours, sharing each other's secrets. They left, leaving the evidence for me to take to the bottle bank!

I still call it my tea house, as I paid for it with some unexpected back pay. It replaced the child's Wendy house and the play frames that were set in a child's garden and vegetable plot. We used to walk down the garden on raining days, to tell stories, paint and draw and walk with umbrellas and wellies 'Singing in the rain'. Sometimes you needed to just get out of the house. I later upgraded to an adult sized house. Luxury! Our friends were already well into this space.

For me my new tea house was my retreat. Set at the back of the garden in the midst of the trees and shrubs. I put in underfelt under lino so it was warm and would not matter if the floor got muddy. We could always brush it out. It got the name as my tea house as I would retreat there after a working day with a cup of tea in the garden. By late afternoon the windows had trapped the warmth and it felt like a safe cocoon. As dusk fell the lighted candles gave it a sense of Karma, surrounded by the sounds of nature and listening to the birds in the hedgerow behind it. Black birds cheeping, squirrels rattling their tails. Connecting calls from parent and offspring. Sometimes I would have a gentle power nap before I was rejuvenated for the evening. Sometimes it was as if I was meditating.

It was a social place too, for early evening drinks. We would start off with a drink and or a starter and then go back inside the house for the rest of the meal. That was the theory. Sometimes we chose to stay outside all night, as the tea house feels special, intimate and a place for friendship and sharing. I have so many happy memories there. We have had curry night starters, antipasto and even parts of a Chinese banquet. However, whatever you wanted was inside the main house, so the tea house gained it's own back shelving, with bottle openers and unbreakable glasses. We abandoned the kettle and fridge as it was just as easy to walk down the garden with drinks.

In many ways my tea house fitted the Danish sense of Hygge. This is all about the experience rather than material stuff. Some think a Hug comes from the Danish Hygge. This includes a mixture of candles and friendship as well as sharing stories about ideas, history, culture and things we create. To me it is part of my home and my family memories.

Looking through the tea house window, and window boxes filled with annuals, you could see the large pink blooms with yellow centres. This was a memory of my father who had bought this showy paeony from the Chelsea flower show. You can also see a large white rhododendron, in my mother's memory, as she bought it for me. In the border near the door is the burial ground of my cats. Above them are plants with traces of yellow, blue and ginger, fond memories of our treasured pets. I surrounded the house with a touch of Zen, with structural Japanese tree peaonies, fragrant mock orange, philadelphus and honeysuckle that bring delicate scents into the meld as we open the windows. Bamboos in containers keep bad spirits away.

This place changed with the seasons from the welcome start of Spring, to being an extension of the house in Summer. As Autumn unfolded, amidst chills, it was a place to still enjoy the last vestiges of growth and the colours of Autumn. The tea house formed a shelter from smoke and the elements on Bonfire night, and in Winter a place to still retreat to if the weather allowed. It would then lay dormant until the start of Spring when the doors and windows would be flung open, the tea house emptied, and the cobwebs and dust and dusty musty smells evicted. I would even clean the windows and wash the cushions and table cloth in readiness for the New Year.

When I retired, the tea house came into its own once again. In daytime it was an essential resting spot during a day's gardening. I never seemed to be able garden all day like I used to. Many afternoons I would soak up the suns warmth and happily nap in my own peace. But it was mainly my favourite creative space. I could write stories in my mind as I dug and weeded. When I rested I would jot down the precious thoughts to consolidate when I was near a computer. Latterly I would have a lap top and there was no stopping me. The peace and space and light were conducive to thought and worlds on other parallel universes. When you returned to the house it was as if you had been to another world and back.

I got a similar effect when I finally evicted all my art stuff from my spare room to the tea house. In Winter it also became my studio. My studio retreat. This was wonderful as a football widow, I knew I had one and a half hours outside to amuse myself. The tea house light is excellent and I could spread my work out round the chairs and walls. By then I had a range of additional comforts, an electric fire and the radio. Time would disappear as my creativity was left to its own devices. Once done the feeling of satisfaction was immense. I could leave those damp oily offerings in the safety of my tea house, rather than the spare room where guests could brush against them.

Happy days. I loved that space and all that it offered me. I can still feel it and smell it and I am there in my mind even though I can no longer see or reach it. When someone helps me, I go back to the tea house. It is wonderful in Spring, listening to nature and the calls and cheeps of the baby birds in the hedgerow. You can feel the gentle breeze through the open windows and hear the buzz of bees and other insects. I still can't get enough of the place, even though my eyes no longer help me. Maybe when I am gone my ashes will be scattered around and it will remain as my very special place.

Katherine

Ann Packwood

A Little Bit of History Should You Visit Lincoln

Geoffrey Chaucer

Dear People, let me introduce myself. My name is Geoffrey Chaucer. I want to tell you about my sister-in-law, Katherine, who became one of the most important people in England's history.

Katherine's father was a Flemish Knight. When she was fifteen she came to the English court to join her sister Phillipa, my very dear wife, who was a lady-in-waiting to the wife of Edward 111. She had an arranged marriage to Hugh Swynford, a distinguished Knight, and they had three children. As the wife of a Knight she was called to Bolingbroke Castle to serve Blanche, the wife of John of Gaunt, Duke of Lancaster, the third son of Edward 111. After the death of Blanche Katherine became the mistress of John of Gaunt, but as she was still married she felt she couldn't continue with the relationship and returned to her manor at Kettlethorpe in Lincolnshire.

During this period England was at war with France. As a Knight, Hugh was in France where he was killed in Battle. Following his death Katherine was recalled to court to become the governess to John of Gaunt's children. Their affair began again. In time they had four children.

Dear people, at this time England was in turmoil. The Black Death ravaged the country, changing the lives of English people forever. It changed the status of peasants and serfs culminating in the Peasants Revolt in 1381. King Richard 11 was only fourteen and his uncle, John of Gaunt, was the most powerful man in the country. The peasants blamed John for their problems. His chil dren were referred to as the Beaufort Bastards and this, coupled with the increasing criticism of their affair, caused John and Katherine to end their relationship. Once again Katherine returned to her estates.

John then married Constance of Castile. After her death John and Katherine were reunited. This time, determined to be together, they were married in Lincoln Cathedral in 1396. John was still the most powerful man in the country and Katherine became The Duchess of Lancaster. Richard 11, in recognition of John's loyalty, legitimised their children. John and Katherine went on to live happily together until his death in 1400. Katherine then returned to her estates in Kettlethorpe and lived there quietly until her death in 1403.

There, dear people, the story should end, but history has another tale to tell.

After Katherine's death her body was brought to Lincoln. As her son, John Beaufort, 1st Earl of Somerset, slowly led the funeral cortege up the steep cobbled hill to the Medieval Cathedral, its three tall spires reaching up into the sky and visible long before you reach the city, he would have been unaware that his grandson, Henry Tudor, would become King of England.

The fight for the right to the throne of England between the Red Rose of Lancaster and the White Rose of York, known as War of The Roses, had been fought for many years. In 1443 when Henry Tudor from the House of Lancaster began to make his claim on the

English throne through his mother Margaret Beaufort, granddaughter of John of Gaunt, he vowed he would marry Elizabeth of York, niece of Richard 111, the reigning King of England.

The two armies of Henry Tudor and Richard 111 met in Bosworth Field, Leicester, in 1445. Richard's army was defeated. Henry became the last English King to win the throne in Battle and Richard became the last English King to die in Battle.**

Henry Tudor became King Henry V11 of England. He married Elizabeth of York in 1446, thus ending the War of the Roses. They were married for 24 years.

So, dear people, should you visit Lincoln I hope that you find the time to visit the Cathedral and stand for a moment or two by Katherine's tomb and reflect on her life. Of humble birth, she became the ancestor of the Tudors and all Kings and Queens of England, through to your present reigning monarch, Queen Elizabeth 11.

** When Richard was killed in Bosworth Fields his body was taken to Grey Friars Church, Leicester, where it lay for hundreds of years. Always intrigued by the story of Richard 111, Phillipa Langley, of the Richard 111 Society, together with a team of archaeologists, set out to discover the remains of Richard. From past records they found that Grey Friars Church had long disappeared and that a car park now stood in its place. With permission to excavate the site the archaeologist began their dig in 2012 and in August 2012 a skeleton was discovered. To prove that the skeleton was Richard 111 extensive research was carried out to ascertain if there were any living descendants. Eventually two relatives were found, their ancestry being traced back to Richard's sister. They were able to provide DNA samples, which were compatible with Richard's, thus confirming that the skeleton was in fact the body of King Richard 111.

The funeral for King Richard 111 took place in March 2015. The funeral procession followed the route from Bosworth Fields to Leicester Cathedral, where Richard's body was interned with all the pomp and ceremony fit for a King of England.

Any historical discrepancies found are down to me – for which I apologise – Ann Packwood

Acknowledgement: Life of Geoffrey Chaucer – Author and Poet.

Fishing boat

Maud Harris

The boy looked out to sea. Alone on the shore, the ozone smell strong in his nostrils, gulls wheeled and soared above him and mist obscured the horizon. A chill wind lifted his fair hair and whipped around his knees. Toby wished he were old enough to wear long trousers
How long he had been standing there, he didn't know; most days he wandered down to the cove, deserted now in the winter season. Where does the sea end, he wondered, does it go on forever? It certainly went as far as his young eyes could see. It had been three weeks now since the fishing boat had set out. Three long weeks. Yet still he expected to see the red sails appear on the horizon, hear the cheerful shout and be swept up and swung around by strong arms. Autumn had morphed into winter, the sea had changed from blue to grey – the wind colder, more cruel, and still Toby waited.

A tiny dot in the vast expanse of water, the boat drifted, becalmed. The storm had come suddenly out of a clear sky. The great tornado venting it's fury as it ripped out the sails. Panic tightened Adrian's chest, he struggled with the controls as a huge wave engulfed the deck.
His partner, Bill, was furiously bailing water, the veins in his neck standing out, his muscles aching from competing with the deluge. All day and all night the vengeful and unrelenting Gods of the sea wreaked their fury.
Then came the calm.
The two fishermen, exhausted, lay back in the boat, the engine torn from its housing by the force of the water, the sails shredded, hanging loose. The sea, which had raged and foamed just hours

before now lay as silk. The blue/green ripples reflecting the sunlight in shimmering patterns. Adrian reckoned their food supplies would last a week if they were careful, but anyway, they would be rescued long before that. Surely a passing ship would see them and come to the rescue? Surely the alarm would be sent out when they didn't arrive home? A week passed; hope wrestled with black despair as night followed day with no sign of help.
Down in the hold Bill struggled with the engines' housing. It lay below deck bent by the force of the water.
 The rations wouldn't last another week and the fresh water, if used sparingly, may last another ten days.
'But we will be seen and rescued before then, won't we?'
The question hung in the air, neither man daring to voice their concerns.
Bill, his face haggard, his beard salt encrusted, grew more morose as the days wore on with no sign of help, and with the food supply dwindling rapidly. He grew more and more manic as his attempts at repairing the damaged engine failed. Frantic now, he paced the deck, muttering to himself through cracked lips, his eyes sunken in his pale face.
The tenth day saw Bill, at midnight, sitting in the bows, he appeared calm, detached, gazing into the middle distance, he was listening intently, rocking to and fro as if to music. The fluorescent water gleamed with myriads of algae, phosphorescent; their pinpricks of light reflecting the stars as far as the eye could see.

Adrian heard nothing.
He climbed the ladder up to the deck.

"Come on, mate, I'll watch and you get some rest."

"Can you hear her?"

Bill turned his haggard face to Adrian, madness in his eyes.

Adrian scanned the dark ocean.

"Hear who?"

"That young girl, she's calling to us, beckoning."

"Bill, mate, there's nobody there."
Bill, stubborn now.

"I know what I can see. "

"Come on now, let's get you down to the bunk, you haven't slept for four nights."
As Adrian went to lead Bill to the ladder he turned, furious, and landed a punch on Adrian's jaw that stunned him.

"For Christ's sake, man, you're hallucinating."

Bill launched himself at Adrian, a heavy spanner in his hand, as Adrian, fighting for his life, grabbed a metal bar and laid Bill out cold on the deck. Manhandling his semi conscious shipmate down to the bunk, Adrian covered him with a blanket.
Choking down the despair that threatened to engulf him, Adrian settled himself down for the night. The moon through the porthole cast a blue glow over everything, the atmosphere seemed charged with electricity. Adrian supposed it must be some phenomenon coupled with the phosphorescent sea.
In other circumstances he could have appreciated the beauty of the scene, but here, with virtually no food and just two days supply of fresh water left, Adrian gave in to despair and wept. He fell into an exhausted sleep, fitfully tossing and turning, waking up bathed in sweat. What awoke him, he didn't know, but a feeling of dread such as he had never known engulfed him. Bill's bed was empty. The ladder up to the deck was slippery with slime, the smell of

rotting fish pervaded his nostrils. Gripping the ladder firmly, he climbed on to the deck. The air was heavy with a sea mist, and the moon cleaved a path through the water.
Bill was nowhere to be found. A battered straw hat floated on the swell.
The Siren had claimed her first victim.

The heavens echoed with Adrian's' cry, his fists raised skywards he roared out his grief and shock.
Alone now in a boat with no sail and a days supply of water, Adrian lay down on the deck and awaited his fate. Haggard and weak with hunger, the worst thing was the thirst. His tongue swollen, his lips cracked and bleeding, he sweltered by day and froze at night. Strange images floated in his tortured mind. In the hinterland between waking and sleeping he heard a soft voice calling him, the song was haunting, sweet and disturbing. It sang in a strange language of peace and calm. Adrian didn't understand the words, but he knew the message they conveyed.
 Staggering to his feet, he made to follow the sound.
From the depths of his dwindling consciousness an inner voice shrieked.
'Don't listen to her, she's not real.'

But still the Siren voice persisted. His face streaked with tears, Adrian threw himself down on the deck and covered his head with a blanket blocking out sound and sight. With the last vestiges of his strength, he resisted the voice.

Joan walked down to the cove, Toby, her son stood in the same place, looking out to sea, he had refused to move from the spot; still he expected to see the red sails appear. Joan gently put her arm around his shoulders. Tears brightened her eyes.

"Come on son, there's nothing more we can do. Your dad and Uncle
Bill won't be coming back."

Toby clenched his fists.

"Yes they will, I know they will."
His jaw set, the child refused to cry.

"Go away, Mam. I'm staying here until they come home."

The deck of the boat reeked with the smell of mouldering nets; Adrian, unconscious now, lay motionless in the bows. He didn't see the yellow helicopter on the horizon, he didn't hear the drone of its engine. He was oblivious to the voice of the medic and the rope ladder lowered from the hovering craft.
Back on dry land, young Toby finished his vigil.

The Future

Jan Parnham

It was a cold crisp early morning, a clear blue sky as Anthony walked briskly up along the well trodden path leading up to the Houghgils. In the far distance he could see snow covering the peaks – it looked peaceful, calm and isolated, which was what he needed at this time in his life. He was staying with his old Etonian friend near Sedbough and had decided to go for a long early walk before breakfast. So he had donned his boots, waxed coat, picked up his faithful stick and set off.

Anthony Henry Cuthbert Smythson was now the head of the family and master of his late father's estate in Norfolk. He was in his late twenties, hoping to travel, further his knowledge and studies in marine life. But his father suddenly dying in a riding accident just over a year ago had put an end to his travelling; he was now left to run the vast estate in Norfolk, and the house which housed his mother, three sisters and a younger brother. Six estate administration staff, estate manager, gardeners, a carpenter. Stable staff and many farm workers also lived there with their own families in cottages on the estate. It was mostly arable land with some sheep and a few special rare breed pigs. So Anthony was now left with a heavy load of over a hundred lives who relied on the land, which had been in his family for over four hundred years.

Then there was Christabella. A beautiful family friend he had known since he was a boy, whom the family had always believed would become his future wife as she was from a good aristocratic background, wealthy landed gentry, which in turn would unite the families fortune. Anthony was fond of 'Christi', as she was sometimes called, but not in love with her- so yet another problem he had to sort out. His mind was so full that he had decided to get away for a week, stay at a friends and spend some time deciding what his next move would be. He came from a privileged background, no money worries, plenty of friends and freedom – until now. Every decision he would now make had huge consequences on many lives – he felt he was not up to the job and the responsibility it entailed – but who else would do it?

He'd been walking now for nearly an hour, he was nearing the snow belt on the hills. There before him was a carpet of crisp pure white snow – he suddenly felt like a big kid wanting to run and play in the virgin snow, making footprints, patterns and roll in it like he did when he was young – feel free without a worry in the world! So that's just what he did. It was wonderful, it was soft, cold on his face as he sank into the fresh snow; he suddenly felt alive. He rolled about, slid, made snowballs to see how far he could throw them and made patterns on the carpet of snow. Suddenly his foot kept falling
And stopped abruptly on the hard ground, then the rest of his body followed, ending up twisted on a hole about six feet deep. For a few moments he froze, then pain came from his ankle area, then his hip; pain gradually crept up his left side. What the hell was he going to do now? He attempted to pull himself out, but because of the thick snow he was unable to get hold of anything to pull himself up and out of the hole.

The pain was kicking in now – perhaps this would be a way out – I would be found frozen, all my problems solved, I could join my father. 'Pull yourself together, you fool. Fight it and look forward to living a full and useful life instead of feeling in sorry for yourself. I'm young and strong and can make a difference.' Now, what next? Did I bring my mobile – he fumbled as best he could in his pocket, it was awkward, but he'd got it. Will there be a signal –

may the Gods be with me, he thought and managed to press the pad. Nothing. He tried again, held the phone up as high as he could. It started to ring, thank God. The housekeeper answered the phone. He shouted, he was injured and trapped in a hole up in the hills. He had taken the path near his friend's house, so hopefully he would be found.

Now he just had to wait. The pain was just about bearable, the snow, cold and shock was starting to numb him, which seemed to actually help. He must have passed out for a time, how long he didn't know, but felt soft snow on his face – his senses arose again, he started to worry that if it snowed any heavier his footprints would be lost, also the hole he was in would start to fill again. Fear crept into his mind. If he did die, what would happen to his family? The shock of his father's death nearly broke his mother's will to live. If he should die – the thought really frightened him – he had to be positive, he had enormous responsibilities which he would honour, follow in his father's footsteps – if he got out of the hole he was in.

He started to plan for the future, he had a very close friend, Simon, whom he trusted totally. He would ask him to join him in the running of the estate and help in planning for the future development of the land and functions which would be needed to carry on financing everything. He would also be honest with Christi, hoping they could still be good friends. Once Simon was able to hold the fort, that was, assuming he would say yes, he would take three months a year out and continue his development in marine life work.
Suddenly he heard a dog barking – help had arrived.

Mother Russia

Maud Harris

"Oh, but they were heady days in old St Petersburg - it was called Petrograd then, you see. Banquets that lasted all evening and dancing until dawn. Gold tableware that gleamed under crystal chandeliers, Grand Duchesses in sumptuous dresses of rainbow colours, their escorts immaculate in uniform. Cockade feathers, skin tight trousers with never a wrinkle and chests resplendent with medals. Course after course was served by footmen attentive to every whim and nuance of their masters."
The old man sat, rheumy eyes gazing into the distance; his grizzled beard overhanging his soiled *telogrieka* jacket, gnarled hand gripping his *charka* with a meagre measure of vodka.
"Tell us more dedushka, tell us more." Young Tatiana and Vanya moved nearer, sitting on the floor at his feet, their eyes wide with curiosity. "Tell us about the Terror."
"Ah. I was but a lad then; I remember how terrified we felt as the mob broke down our door, the splintering sound as the locks gave way. The servants were screaming. Baba, my nurse threw herself on top of my sister Saskia, and I hid under her skirts." "What happened then, dedushka, what happened then?" Vanya had heard the tale many times but still he listened, breathless. "Ah! What happened then?" The old man sighed. "It was winter time. And now bow your heads, my children, and be thankful that you will never know cold like it. Baba took us by the hand and rushed out into the snow. Behind us we could hear screams and rifle fire. As we fought our way deeper into the forest we could hear the crackle of flames. Looking back we saw the red glow as our house burned.

Mama and Papa, expecting something like this, had entrusted Baba with a casket containing some of Mama's jewels. These she used to provide money for our escape. Saskia scowled and stamped her feet as Baba took away her silk robes and replaced them with rough homespun garments such as the common peasants wore. 'Now, now, *kotyonok*, we cannot be seen with aristocrat's trappings. Until we reach safety we remain in disguise.' I never minded dressing in homespun worker's gear, as it was an adventure for me. Saskia, who had led the life of a princess was petulant and difficult, just like an older sister.

On and on we went in the bitter cold scavenging food where we could, sometimes bargaining, sometimes stealing; later on we learned through travellers that the mob had dragged the Tsar and Tsarina out and shot them all in cold blood. We knew then we could never go back." At this point *dedushka's* eyes filled with tears and he had to pause.

"Baba led us westward to the mighty Volga river, she bargained with the boatman and, ragged and hungry we boarded the vessel bound for the border and safety. Days we spent on that boat, cramped and sick. Saskia and I had to support Baba, who had grown weak with worry and starvation. Somehow we arrived safely in Italy and were met by a band of ragged Russian escapees. We were taken in and fed the first truly Russian food for months. Baba was allowed to rest and regain her strength before another boat ride - this time on a large, well maintained ship."

Dedushka paused once more, for what seemed an age. To Tatiana and I he seemed lost in a world we could not share. "Tell us about meeting Babushka"

"Ah, Babushka! On the boat was the most beautiful woman I had ever seen. Young as I was I knew at once that she was my future. Milk white skin, dark brown eyes, a smile hovered round the corners of her mouth. She spoke Russian with the same accent as my own. I knew without a doubt that all the hardship had been leading to this. It was Karma." Dedushka leaned back, his eyes closed. We thought he had fallen asleep. Long minutes passed then he looked earnestly at Tatiana and I.

"And now, with another war looming what will be the future of my beloved Mother Russia? Come let me embrace you, my children."

Translations; telogrieka : a military style Russian jacket
charka: a Russian drinking vessel
kotyonok: kitten.
Dedushka: grandpa
Babushka: grandma.

__Maud Harris__ is a retired nurse. She writes mystery books set around a hospital theme. Her first autobiographical story 'Three Years in Starch' is an account of nurse training in the late 1950s to early 1960s. Having travelled extensively, she is now settled in the Nottingham area.

__Ann Packwood.__ Over 25 years ago Ann wrote her first children's story, to read to her grandson. Seven further stories followed and they were then put away in a cupboard.
The Bingham Writing Group, whilst encouraging her to write short stories, gave her the 'light bulb' moment to get her childrens' stories out again, and this time to share them with other children.

__Brenda Dobson__ lives in Bingham. At school, she loved English and was considered a bookworm. Then, for a while, work got in the way of other pursuits, but she is now retired and enjoys writing for pleasure. The Bingham Writing Group has given her encouragement to put things in print but she doesn't feel confident that she is quite ready yet. She has tried a mix of WEA courses and has written various poems and short stories. She has also tried her hand at Faction, based on her forays into family history and intends that there be more to come, once she has time. Retirement, she says, is busy!

__Desirée Fearon__ has always been interested in writing, and at school was recognised as someone with the potential to become an established author. She writes about the things that interest her and is an inveterate people watcher. This anthology sees her in print for the first time.

Roger Smith worked as a scientist in the food and drug industry for 25 years before changing career to teach about health. Now, being self employed, he is free to share how much healthier we can all be without reliance on processed foods and pharmaceuticals. Rogers writing often reflects his beliefs in the healing properties of: good surroundings, good food and plenty of activity, having a purpose in life, working on relationships and being an example of how to live a clean and healthy life.

Maria Ng Perez is a poet with a lower case 'puh'. She has been writing on and off since her teens, though admittedly, more off than on. She is more of a dabbler and procrastinator, and recognises her lack of discipline, which she intends to address…tomorrow. She also dips her toes in prose and is currently working on developing her knowledge and portfolio in this area. Her writing is eclectic, though she does have a 'thang' for punnery and word play. Most of her work revolves around human interactions, behaviours and emotions, particularly affairs of the heart. She believes that if her crafted words have not affected you emotionally, then she has failed as a writer.

Jan Parnham has worked all her life in advertising, display, exhibition work and photography. She has also done antique furniture restoration and now works part-time in an art gallery. She is married with two children and joined Bingham Writing Group because she wants to write a book about her son, who has Down's Syndrome. She hopes it may help other families with special needs children to talk about all the positive and loving times life can

Pat Bassett I live in Bottesford with my husband. My two daughters have three children between them. I have always enjoyed writing but life has somehow got in the way. Joining the writing group has made me find time to put pen to paper and given me a purpose for doing so.

Made in the USA
Columbia, SC
04 October 2017